I remember Syl
&
Other stories

Malthouse African fiction

I remember Syl
&
Other stories

Valentine Umelo

m althouse λp

Malthouse Press Limited

Lagos, Benin, Ibadan, Jos, Oxford, Port-Harcourt, Zaria

Malthouse Press Limited
43 Onitana Street, near Stadium Hotel Road, Off Western Avenue
Lagos Mainland, Lagos State, Nigeria
E-mail: malthouse_press@yahoo.com
malthouselagos@gmail.com
Tel: +234 (01) -773 53 44; 0802 600 3203

© Valentine Umelo 2009
First Published 2009
ISBN 978 978 8422 02 0

Distributors:

African Books Collective Ltd
Oxford, United Kingdom
Website: http://www.africanbookscollective.com

Special dedication

For my beloved wife, Georgina
Honey, you dreamt with me
Sleep on now, my love

Dedication

To my children:
Michael, Karen, Macedonia and Jedidiah
-    Thanks for being there for me

To my parents and siblings:
-    You have been my rock

To Raliya O. Sanni (Fulani)
and
Abdulganiyu Amoto Ibrahim
-    Thanks for reading through

The stories

1

going home

As soon as breakfast was over that Saturday, the bugle sounded for us to assemble. Doe growled. He had come to loathe the shrill sound of the camp master's metallic instrument, like me. Tired from doing nothing, Doe and I trudged towards the 'Assembly Ground' when the bugle sounded a second time. The 'Assembly Ground' was Solo's christening of the large clearing in the middle of the refugee camp where everyone gathered for announcements.

Already, several refugees had gathered: men and women; the sick, the not-too-healthy, the healthy; the young and the old. Babies strapped to their mothers' backs kicked feebly. They stretched their fragile necks; turned their oversized heads. Here, there, everywhere. As if the piece of information anticipated was specifically meant for them. They too were fed up with refugee life, having all been conceived and born as refugees.

I was surprised to behold the familiar fleshy face of the big white man, Mr. Stevenson. Why, it was less than three months ago that he was here. He was having troubles keeping his rubbery smile in place. Did he have to look so nervous? With his shiny bald patch, protruding tummy and the sweat streaming down his face, I thought of an amateur jester whose opening act had gone sour. Because it was his duty to bring the file all the way from Monrovia, this quiet, soft-spoken, clumsy-looking white man was the Messiah everyone had been thirsting for.

As usual, the atmosphere hummed with uncertainty. Dust from hurrying feet rose high into the morning air. The humidity was palpable. Doe's tongue hung out, limp; his foamy spittle dripping as he shadowed me.

"Quickly, quickly," old Bobo, the camp master was calling. "Come over here everyone."

He beckoned in every direction, with both hands, the ominous thin blue file firmly in place under his left armpit. Justice Mamburay was standing miserably in the back, not expecting to hear his name. Perhaps he was preparing to carry out his threat. I felt sorry for him. I approached him, determined not to let him out of my sight.

"Nobody has to cry or behave as if the end has come," old Bobo began.

"You've all fared well since you came to this camp years ago. Have I treated you poorly? Tomorrow is heavily pregnant. If you don't hear your name today, there is still tomorrow." There is still tomorrow indeed! He could say that again. Let him pretend that all was well. After all, was he a refugee? Did he know how it felt, thinking that your name would never appear on the sheaf of document inside that blue file; that your entire family members were probably all dead; that you would probably spend the rest of your life living in a refugee camp? There is still tomorrow indeed!

He flipped the blue file open. Chests rose in huge measures; exhaled deeply. Time stood still. A name I couldn't hear clearly floated through the air. A loud cry broke out in the middle of the crowd. It was Geraldine Kpakpor, that stout and formidable character. Not wishing to be knocked down and out, people hastily made way as Geraldine pounded forward to that elevated spot where she knew she should be. Having partaken in this horrible ritual over and over again, that spot, which Geraldine now commanded, had become so desirable, like gold. Everyone dreamt of the day that it would be his turn to stand there. I had stood there over a million times - in my endless nightmares.

Old Bobo kept reading out more and more names. He even called Justice Mamburay. I watched enviously (and relieved at the same time) as Justice tore to the sacred spot like a tornado. Tears of joy ran down his sunken cheeks. Whether from hearing his name, or from the fact that he would no longer have to carry out his threat, I would never know.

After about an hour of such tension-filled drama in which members of the cast yelled, cried, rolled on the ground, some collapsing, old Bobo, the main actor began closing his thin file. The horror script had come to an end: no more bloodletting; no more names to be read out. I smiled bitterly. Nobody had recognised me, again. I would not be going home.

I turned to stalk away. From the corner of my eyes, I saw heads turning to seek me out. Later I would recall that I had heard that voice the first and even the second time. But I had paid no attention to it. I became aware of it as it called out a third and fourth time.

"Trueman!"

"Cyprian Trueman!"

The camp master had kept this best for last. For I of the depressed mind had become quite popular in camp. His voice kept rising and falling as it called out my name. And with this sweet voice arose certain difficulties. All these months, I had pre-occupied my mind with hearing my name read out; with thoughts of going home. I had paid lip-service to that part of the equation that said, What if I got home to discover that...?

2

Going home

Now that reality struck me. Could I face the disturbing possibilities; the changes that I might encounter when I got home? Instantly, I was afraid of leaving the safety of this humble refugee camp where over the years, my life had established a steady, easy rhythm. Why, I had grown into a man in it. Was I prepared to begin life afresh? Was I prepared to face new challenges? Since I couldn't take him with me to Liberia, to whom would I abandon Doe, my three-legged dog?

Who would meet me at the airport, my pa or my ma? How big were Dupsey and Josiah and Olla now? Suddenly, I recalled Dupsey's ebony black hair and round, clear eyes and my eyes smarted. Most especially, I thought, Will they all still be alive? Or will I get home and be told that so and so and so had died during the war? I also wondered about my Uncle Mel. I recalled his pained voice as he cried that day the rebels struck, 'Go on C.Y., run, and don't bother about me. I'll be alright.' Was he all right? My mind was filled with scary thoughts. Was I to remain in the camp the rest of my life, or go back home? I wasn't sure anymore which I wanted.

Doe knew I was going home. The moment I broke down and began to cry after old Bobo's voice finally got my attention, he slunk away. Poor dog, the script had come out differently this time. In other circumstances in the past when my name was omitted, it was he, Doe, who licked away my tears. He stuck with me as I found a suitable place to drown my sorrows.

On the day Solo left, he was my rock. Solo's name had come up during the third name-calling seven months ago. His was among fifteen other names that came up. It seemed as if I would die. My best friend was going home. My best friend was leaving me behind.

Solo didn't jump, like others whose names were called. But I knew he was overjoyed to be going home after nine years in a refugee camp in a foreign country, separated from family and friends. His face shone. His gait changed. He tried to disguise it all. He knew I was feeling bad. All through that day, he did his best to console me. It was a wasted effort.

I thought, What injustice. After nine whole years together, why should we suddenly be given less than twenty-four hours to be with each other, then to be separated, perhaps, forever? I counted the seconds. By evening when the Bedford bus that would bear his set of returnees to Conakry, en route to Monrovia by air arrived, I had already gone to pieces. It felt as if my heart was being torn out; as if life's very essence was being drained from me.

When morning came, Solo and I clasped each other, hugging so tight we almost choked. It took the combined effort of two camp elders to tear us apart. For their troubles, Doe, as sad as I was sank his canines into one's ankles. As his bus sighed out of camp, Solo wept loudly, waving with all

3

his strength.

"Bye, bye C.Y.," he choked again and again. "Just as I heard my name, that's how you'll hear your own name one day." After Solo left, I didn't have any more interest in shoemaking, which earned us much-needed income. Out of frustration, I changed from my good ways. I took to raiding the surrounding farms. I dug up immature carrots. Carted away any eatable I could find. Just for the fun of it. Local women cursed me for marching through their farms, destroying young seedlings of cassava, maize and vegetables. They spat on me in broad daylight. I was too frustrated to care.

I lost track of time. Without Solo, there was no time. Everyday, I thought of my family and missed Solo. I didn't care so much for the company of the other boys in camp. The truth was that I wasn't such a good mixer. People felt sorry for me, seeing the way I was carrying on, alone and depressed. I felt sorry for myself too. I knew this wasn't the right thing to do, feeling sorry for myself the way I did. But there was nothing I could do about it.

Solo had meant so much to me. He was like the elder brother I didn't have. In camp, he had played the role of a father, a mother and a best friend. He was the reason I got out of bed everyday since the past nine years. We had been thrown into adjacent seats on the lorry that evacuated us from the holding camp in Monrovia as we made our journey out of Liberia, en-route to becoming Internationally Displaced Persons. That was how he began taking care of me. Now that he had waved his goodbye and was gone, how would I manage? Solo crying and waving goodbye the way he did! That was the second time someone who meant so much to me was departing in a like manner. The first time had seen me separated from my family all these nine years.

With Doe on my heels, I rushed into our hall. I gaped at Solo's corner, as though hoping to see him lying there, like he had all these years. Doe sniffed everywhere, hoping to ferret him out. But like an empty post-office box, his corner echoed loudly, reminding me more than anything else that I was truly alone. Doe, God bless his soul. He consoled me, licking away my tears. What would I have done without that disabled dog?

Doe knew all about pain. If only he could talk. At puppyhood, he had lost his right leg to a metal trap and his mother abandoned him to the elements in a rice field where Solo and I found him shivering, dying. By sheer tenacity, we had nursed him back to life. Then Solo left him. And now, I was preparing to abandon him as well!

Unlike other nights when I made sure he slept outside, when Doe insisted on coming in to lie beside me this night, I let him. The men and

4

boys in my hall understood. They didn't mind his coming into the hall to sleep, they said. In a way, Doe belonged to us all, even though he had always been referred to as, "Solo and C.Y.'s dog". Later in the night when I opened my eyes, he was still wide-awake. He was shivering. It wasn't from the night's cold.

In the morning, I felt his cold nose nuzzling my face and woke up. As I did my toilet, he trailed after me, licking and licking, as though I was a day old puppy. His bright eyes never left mine. The pain I felt seeing him so sad, God! It was worse than the pain of toothache. Eventually I had to speak to both the camp master and Mr. Stevenson.

"Doe, my dog is suffering," I told them, holding back tears. Then I let the tears flow. I loved Doe so much as to be ashamed of crying for him. Doe was by my side. Both men saw what I meant. Doe's whimpers were loud enough for a stone deaf to hear. Doe scanned the ground nervously. I swallowed hard as I watched his slumped shoulders. Old Bobo who never displayed any emotion was touched. His moustache twitched nervously.

"But you know you can't take him with you," he said after his twitching had subsided. It seemed as if Doe had heard the ugly verdict. Painful whimpers escaped from him. "But don't worry," old Bobo consoled me. "I'll make sure he is well taken care of."

"Are you sure, Bossman?" I cried.

"I am sure he will look after your dog well," Mr. Stevenson said kindly.

"Doe doesn't like bulgur wheat at all at all," I explained amidst tears, which were blinding me now.

"I'll give him whatever he likes best," old Bobo assured me.

Though I didn't trust old Bobo to take good care of Doe, there was nothing I could do but pray that he at least showed my poor dog the littlest consideration; that he didn't use his stick on him. I bundled my Doe away as both old Bobo and Mr. Stevenson watched.

At about eight o'clock when the bell of the Catholic Church a kilometre or so away began to peal for the second mass, our journey back home commenced. I was the last to board. I wanted to spend as much time as I could with Doe, rubbing his head. But the hour of reckoning finally came. Doe didn't struggle to enter the bus. When old Bobo barred the door with a stick after I got in with my back, a low whine escaped him. Not wishing to lose sight of me, he marched a few paces backwards, his eyes searching mine, questioning; his whole body quivering. Sitting down, he began wagging his stump of a tail. The very trap that had amputated his right leg had left him with a stump for a tail. He wagged his stump slowly at first and then madly as the bus began to inch away. Then as the bus gained speed, Doe began chasing; limping and limping and limping. It was

5

the race of his life. It was so much of an effort to keep from stumbling. Then he stumbled, burying his head in the dust, his legs cycling in the air as he involuntarily kept chasing. I sank my head in my hands. Some of my fellow returnees sobbed too. So, they too had secretly loved Doe, I thought. Solo and I could have let them play with him more often than we allowed. But it was too late now.

I thought, Would Doe ever go back to that camp? Perhaps my going would give him the chance to pursue his own life. I hoped he found himself a lovely mate. But I didn't see how. With his disabilities, he couldn't compete; with his disabilities he didn't stand a chance in hell in the world of animals where 'unconditional love' and 'love by pity' did not exist. But he was a lovely creature: thick, dirty brown fur, shrunken right leg, stumped tail and all.

I sat next to Justice Mamburay. Justice Mamburay was my age, seventeen. He had said, "If they don't call my name next time, I will kill myself." That was at the last name calling three months ago when old Bobo read out the names of those to be repatriated and his name wasn't there. After we had driven for several hours and thoughts of Doe had receded from most minds, I let my hand drop lightly on his shoulder. He turned and smiled at me, shyly. I could see that he was embarrassed, but relieved to be still alive.

I had appreciated Justice's point of view, but hadn't particularly subscribed to it. I wasn't going to commit suicide or do anything as stupid. I had spent all these years in a refugee camp trying to stay alive. In the hope that one day, I would be re-united with my family. I was hungry to find out about my Uncle Mel. Shrapnel from an exploding grenade had stuck into his thigh and he was bleeding. It was the peak of the dry season. We had gone for a mid-day swim at a nearby stream when the rebels struck. Did he make it to safety after urging me on with shouts of, 'Go on C.Y.'

I wanted to hug again my little sister, Dupsey, three years old then. Nine years had gone by since! She would be a big girl now, a lady. I wanted to tell her certain things. Like how I loved her so much and would never desert her again. Like I did that afternoon when she begged to go with Uncle Mel and I to the stream and I had said a capital, 'NO' and she had kept crying and waving and shouting, 'Good bye, good bye.' It was believed that children were spirits and could commune with spirits. In her child / spirit's eye, did she somehow know we were being separated, perhaps for good? This thought had plagued my mind over the years. I wanted to tell her how I had thought about her every single day since. I equally wanted to tell her about this disturbing dream I had been having repeatedly in recent months. In the dream, she wouldn't let me play with her, crying instead, 'Go away, go away. You don't belong with me.' Perhaps she was still angry with me for deserting her. I must ask her forgiveness. It would not be like my business with Solo where I couldn't find time to say a simple 'thank you', for his friendship and his love after all these nine years. As we rode along the bumpy highway to Conakry, I kept thinking, A year and six months. That is what it had taken for this 'blessed Sunday' to come for us. We had believed that by simply being photographed a year and half ago, we were on our way home. But we were wrong. For almost a year, nothing happened to ensure we went home; fresh fighting kept erupting in Liberia: today Lofa County, tomorrow Nimba County, the next day the border between Liberia and Ivory Coast. We continued to be refugees, residing in a camp in Nzerekore, a border town in Guinea Conakry.

All that waiting seemed to have been in another lifetime now.

Those photographs taken of us had been made into an album by the UNHCR and nailed at the Capitol in Monrovia. The public had been viewing them since. With the hope that some of us in this and other camps scattered around the boarder with Guinea, Sierra Leone and Ivory Coast; and even as far as Ghana and Mali would be spotted by those still alive amongst our relatives. If you were lucky to be spotted, you went home. Otherwise, you continued to reside in the camp. We had left hundreds who have not been identified still at the camp. Perhaps some would remain there forever, given the brutality of our civil war.

Monday morning was for being counselled at the UNHCR in Conakry and resting off the fatigue of the long, arduous bus ride from Nzerekore. Tuesday morning we boarded a UN chartered flight.

Five hours into the journey, I felt emptiness in the pit of my stomach as the plane descended swiftly. Below was the city of Harbel. The sight before me was frightening. Everywhere I turned canopies and tents confronted me. With the inscribed UNHCR emblem easily visible on them even from the sky, they seemed to occupy every available space. What had happened to all the houses?

When the aeroplane's door was thrown open, the blast of dry, hot wind couldn't keep any of us from rushing outside. We were eager to embrace the Fatherland. There were temporary shacks everywhere. The only semblances of solid buildings were ripped apart in places. Numerous bullet holes riddled their walls, making ugly zigzag patterns. Lizards wriggled in and out of the holes.

The immigration officers who welcomed us were a sharp contrast to their confident, happy, well-dressed counterparts in Conakry. These ones were clothed in misery.

I may have been terribly shocked at the destruction in the airport of Harbel. But there are no adequate words to explain how I felt, or what I saw as we entered Monrovia. Whatever I am able to say in these few written words is just a tip of the despair that met my eyes. Even the most gifted photographer would fail to capture it all on film!

Inch after inch of the city had been crushed. Houses had been gutted down by fire and blown away with bombs and rocket propelled grenades. People crawled out of tents to cheer us: children with protruding stomachs and thin legs evident of kwashiorkor; adults with sunken eyes, bony skulls and wrinkled, scaly skins. They all waved at us enthusiastically, with what strength they had. Compared to the Monrovia I had fled from, this was a living nightmare, a scene from hell! As we approached our destination, I couldn't help but say a silent prayer:

"Dear God, may Liberia never experience another war again. Amen!"

No relatives awaited us at the UNHCR headquarters when we arrived around two o'clock. No announcement of our arrival had been made in order to avoid all the tension and commotion associated with the arrival of returning refugees, especially children and teenagers.

We rested and were given some light refreshment. Around four o'clock when the heat of the blazing, Monrovian sun had subsided, our reunification with our families began. For about fifteen minutes, we kept cruising. When the vehicle went past the magnificent Colonel Muammar Gaddafi building in Sinkor, I could hardly recognise it. It was a pitiable mass of injured bricks and all. It must have burnt for days, for every inch of it was covered with soot. Only the skeletal framework remained as evidence that such a wonderful building had ever existed. My mind went back to the good old days when I used to ride on its fine lift with my sisters and brother and Uncle Mel.

"Cyprian Trueman?"

"Bossman?" I answered, coming back to reality.

I stared at the official accompanying us.

"You'll go first."

"Me?"

"Yes."

"But Bossman, we live in Paynesville," I protested, "not Sinkor."

"Your folks have relocated to Sinkor now."

"Oh..."

I had the sudden urge to urinate. The van turned into a side street after the Monrovia City Hall, now a mass of fallen bricks and all, a caricature of its former imposing self. It was a dusty street filled with potholes.

And then I noticed the crowd in front of a house further down. As we got closer, I saw that like the other houses we had passed, an explosion had blown off its roof. In its place was a UNHCR white tarpaulin, secured in places by bricks and sticks. The same tarpaulins covered the doors and windows, serving as curtains. Already, there was a UNHCR jeep in front of the house. An advance team had come to meet my family, and to prepare them for my homecoming. I strained my neck as I made my way out of the van. And then I saw her. She had shrunk in size, like meat after passing through a roaring flame. She wore a yellow blouse. A blue, threadbare wrapper secured her waist. I stared at her face. It was the face of an ugly, old woman that stared back. However, in those shining, eyes filled with gratitude, and love, I still recognised my poor mother!

Standing beside her in an old, white, singlet and brown trousers was my father. Seeing me step down from the van, he pretended to be smiling, even though tears were streaming from his wrinkled eyes.

"Mr. Trueman, be ashamed of yourself," one of the advance team of UNHCR officials rebuked. "This isn't the way to receive your son after all these years. I thought we had agreed there would be nothing like this."

My father nodded, meaning that he too thought that the original arrangement was that there would be nothing like shedding of tears.

"Mr. Trueman, be happy to see your son."

"You should all be smiling."

"He is alive."

"Stop this, madam. Be happy."

"We're happy," my father, amidst tears told the UN officials who were by now clearly annoyed at the morbid shape an otherwise simple process was assuming.

"I'm smiling," my mother choked, revealing all her teeth as she tried to prove she was smiling. Two front lower teeth were missing. I sighed. My once, beautiful mother!

A thin boy and an equally thin girl were lurking in my parent's shadows. Suddenly, they sprang forward, as our eyes met.

"Our C.Y., our C.Y.," they yelled at the same time, hugging me. Unlike my brother and sister who rushed to hug me, my parents simply beheld me.

"Our C.Y., mi name Olla," my sister said in our Liberian style English.

"Mi name Josiah," my brother said, as if on cue.

I was blank. Or so it seemed, for Josiah suddenly asked:

"You can't remember we?"

I choked as I told him I remembered them all right. But something wasn't quite right. I couldn't see her. Could she have run a little errand for our mother? It would be just like her, ever so kind. She used to give away her meat and fish when we ate together those days when we were kids. I looked around for the girl I had always known with jet-black hair and round laughing eyes. Oh how I loved her. I swallowed hard, and it hurt so much. My throat was just too dry. The question I wanted to ask stuck in it. But I managed it all the same.

"Where...where is our Dupsey?"

The whole place became dead silent. As if a ghost had just strolled past. Some people looked into the far distance. Others stared down, embarrassed. Standing before me, my father bit his fingernails. Helplessly, my mother wiped a tear, which was quickly replaced by another and another and another. Someone blew his nose. Another cleared his throat. I searched faces. People averted their faces in haste.

"I can't see her, our Dupsey," I yelled at last, smashing the silence. "And our Uncle Mel, too. He was wounded in the stream. Didn't he come home?"

"Shift back, all of you," a voice, which sounded familiar, said. "Give the boy some air."

The crowd shuffled back just far enough to give the impression of shifting back. The muttering which commenced when I yelled for our Dupsey rose and fell in rhythm, like a death song. In the distance, a bicycle bell clanged.

"Look Cyprian," the voice said again, firmly this time, as the owner stepped forward to take control. "Be patient. You will get all the answers later. I said give the boy some air."

I was momentarily taken aback. Before me was Mr. Stevenson, every muscle in his fleshy face taut. What had happened to that smiling Mr. Stevenson, the one I used to know? This Mr. Stevenson was stern, even unfriendly. Gone were his sloppy manners; gone were his unsure demeanours; gone was his pasted smile. Then it struck me. Mr. Stevenson was the leader of the reunification team. He had been observing events calmly from a distance all these while. And had only been forced out when it appeared that his subordinates were messing up things. He looked mean, towering belligerently above his colleagues. I felt a shiver run through me. And suddenly I was angry with everyone and everything - Mr. Stevenson, his unprofessional colleagues, my beaten parents, my wasted life as a refugee, the senseless war, Solo's absence, Doe's predicament, everything.

"I want all the answers now," I exploded, crumbling into my mother's now outstretched arms. There in her bosom, I sobbed my heart out, for our Dupsey and our Uncle Mel.

2

i remember Syl

Banjul, The Gambia.
October 24, 200-.
3:07 p.m.

(i)

My dear Joe,

Ol' boy, how you dey? How bodi? You well? Long time no see. Na wa o! Unbelievable, my dear Joe! Your letter and the accompanying package came as a complete surprise, a bolt from the blue to say the least. Christ, the power of the Internet is truly immense. It is mammoth. My junior brothers sent that 'namedatabase' thing to my inbox, urging me to register. It took me several days gravitating, 'should I register? Should I not register?' Even as I sat before the screen contemplating, I saw the number of people registering rising: 7, 876, 765; 7, 876, 766; 7, 876, 767; ...and, at last, I was compelled to, after all, if you can't beat them, join them!

How was I to know that you would search that website some day and find my name and address listed? Ahhh, I thank God for your letter, and especially for you, my dear friend. Your letter meant so much to me, and the things you sent ...I love and appreciate them sooooo much. Thank you.

Joe, tell me, do you miss The Gambia, even slightly? Do you (though, as you once put it, they lack our culinary expertise and variety) miss their dishes? That jollof rice – *benachin* - of the Wolofs, which is prepared with chicken, beef or fish, seasoned with salt, black pepper, garlic, vinegar and then fried with onions; *domodah*, of the Mandinkas, which is tasty, pasty light brown groundnut sauce, with which boiled rice is eaten; *sowe*, of the Fulas, which is fresh cow milk, made sour and curdly after being left overnight in calabashes to beautifully ferment, becoming *chakri* when mixed and eaten with couscous (millet flour).

You used to enjoy *fufu* of the Akus, which is cassava cooked and pounded after it had been soaked in water and allowed to ferment and soften for three or four days, and then eaten with super *kanja*, palm oil sauce made from fresh okra and cooked with fresh or smoked fish. What of *plasas*, that vegetable sauce of potato or cassava or *krin-krin* leaves. Ahhh, your mouth is watering I know, I know. And *ogiri*, locust bean upon fermentation, offensive smelling, yet unbeatable, without which pepper soup would lose its wonderful aroma, and tantalizing flavour? Do you recollect it all?

Do you miss the people? The unassuming boys and men, skin, shiny black, tall; and the beautiful girls and women, with their heavy drooping backsides, like...like what now...fully ripe pumpkins, brown, on their way slowing, as if to kiss the earth; their sparkling, even teeth accentuated even more by their coarse, ebony black skins, which you could write white chalk on. Ha, ha, ha...you once told me you would lay down your life, for one of these Gambian women, have you forgotten?

Do you miss the sweet music from such varied traditional instruments as the *riti, balafon, halam, tama, balonbata*, and especially from the fabulous but simple string instrument, the *kora*, of the Mandinkas? Do you, my dear friend, miss the heady tunes from the rusted, but eloquent saxophones of the Jollas; the energetic dancing of the Manjangos?

Do you recall the beautiful hairdos of the Wolofs; and their feet and hands, always dyed deep black with henna?

What of the gay laughter of all and sundry in spite of the cramps in empty stomachs, from hunger; pain from diseases; and sorrow from death?

Do you miss the gleaming white sands of The Gambia's beaches?

Do you miss the shining sun? It is blazing fit to roast outside, as I write, seated astride a long, broad wooden bench in my parlour, facing the ungauzed window. I am trying to look out, but like an albino, I can only squint. The sun's rays, millions and millions of dazzling brilliance, can you imagine, as they are reflected back to the heavens, hauling and shattering themselves, as if in a great penance, upon the corrugated zinc sheets of bungalows? Of course you can, you spent several years here and know the weather as well as I do.

I can only see a couple of goats and rams as everyone is inside sheltering, no one wants to get baked, and one of the goats is bleating now, others have joined in, including the rams...mhhheeee... mhhheeee... baaaa, baaaaa, mhhheeee... Joe, the sun is just too hot, too hot. Four or five years ago, it didn't use to be as hot as this. All this talk about the ozone layer and green house effect and climate change, desertification and Kyoto protocol.

i remember Syl

It is all gobbledygook to me. I wish Syl were here to explain it all to me! Do you remember Syl? And the wind is conspiring with the blazing sun. It is still: like a corpse, like a dead man's secret. Can you hear it? No, of course, you can't, but the waves of the Atlantic are booming, roaring, and crashing thunderously as they rush to shore (as if to deliver an urgent message), and yet there is no wind to fan and cool my face, clean-shaven. Whatever happened to sea breeze, or is it land breeze? You should see the brown sweat dripping down my back, down my sides, tickling my armpits, down my face, into my mouth. I taste it...salty, like seawater...ughhhhhhh.

** **

Yes, my dear friend, I am still here, in The Gambia. To be precise Banjul. If someone had told me that I would be here after ten years, I would have called that person a liar. A big liar! But here I am after ten whole years. Have I made any progress, you would ask? Decide for yourself after reading my letter. It is rather long, an epistle you would say. But I know you are not afraid to read. You always loved reading. What better attestation than those fine Wole Soyinka's plays and Chinua Achebe's novels on your dusty bamboo shelf in our then base, the provincial town of Farafenni, which used to be a whole day's journey from Banjul?

When we...I left Nigeria, the idea then was to use The Gambia as, how did we normally put it, 'A stepping-stone'. Those who were here before us, swearing to the gods, the small gods they worshipped, had told us with certainty that, 'The Gambia is only a stone throw, a whistle, a shout, to Europe. And to bliss, and heaven.' They told us: 'From The Gambia, one can clearly see the yellow and white streetlights burning in Madrid and Brussels. And Luxemburg and Paris. In The Gambia, one can easily feel the vibrations, the tremor of the earth (of the subways) in Oslo and Stockholm and Copenhagen.'

It sounded unbelievable, but we believed, didn't we, and many others? Remember what they told us? 'There is this place in The Gambia called 'German'. From this 'German', one can board a vehicle going to Germany: to Berlin and to Frankfurt. And there is this other place called 'London'. From this 'London', one can get a one-way bus ticket to that great city, London, the capital of the world.'

Well, we found out the truth for ourselves, didn't we? And ten years later, ten whole years after hearing and swallowing hook, line and sinker, those ill intended lies, yours truly is still in The Gambia.

Broken? Wrecked? Frustrated?

13

I leave you to draw your own conclusion. What really hurts me, is that I can't go back home to Nigeria. Tell me, why should I go back, why? The shame will kill me faster than an incurable disease. Can I bear the embarrassment? The insults: 'That's him, a first born, that spent ten years in The Gambia and came back with nothing. He is now searching for a job. His mates are all established. All the while he was away, he couldn't send a pin home to his poor mother. His sisters got married and he was not in attendance at any of their weddings, his brothers went through the university without a single help from him...a complete failure.'

I can hear it all, even now!

I'll not go back, definitely not NOW! Maybe later. You see, even if I wanted to go back, for a short visit, I changed my mind when I remember Syl. Yes, Syl. You know Syl, don't you? Ahhh, there is so much about Syl to tell you, so much.

So how are you, my dear friend? I miss you so much that my heart aches. Your dimpled cheeks, and infectious smile, which brightens the surrounding, like a 100 watts bulb, suddenly switched on. Your ringing laughter, which made chickens cackle; donkeys and horses grazing in the fields exchange quick glances. I miss your jokes, never could tell one myself, unlike you, who like a griot, had such fine jokes and fables.

I miss your brilliantly forged palm-wine drinkers' songs too...especially that one about Caro, the pretty, fair complexioned maiden - 'yellow *Sisi* - who squandered a loving suitor's hard earned money and eloped with a white man -'*Oyibo*- only to have her heart broken:

'...Caro O, yellow *sisi*,
Caro O, na my yellow *sisi* O,
Caro chop my money follow *Oyibo*,
Oyibo run away Caro begin cry:
A jambene a ja, a jambene a ja.'

Ahhhh, my dear friend! You had such fine, easy ways. I miss them so much. The children of Farafenni miss you. They always ask me:

"Where is your fat friend, Jobe?"

They keep calling you Jobe. You always shouted and told them your name wasn't Jobe, but Joe. With your effeminate (no offence meant) fingers, you even had to spell it on the hard, dusty, Farafenni earth, while they watched, dressed in tattered shorts, bare-chested and exposing black gums with several missing teeth or crater-ridden from excess sugar in their breakfasts of Churagerthe and their much-loved Chinese green tea, *ataya*, brewed on locally made coal pots and drank round the clock!

14

"Joe, my name is Joe. J...O...E," you spelt, "Joe! Not Jobe."
"Joe?" they cried, their eyes sparkling as if in sudden possession of a sacred knowledge.
"Yes, JOE, JOE, not JOBE."
But for all your efforts, my dear friend, you achieved nothing because the village children continue to call you Jobe. To them, you would always remain, 'That fat Jobe'. The kids...Ahhh, my dear friend, they are no longer kids. They are now all in their late teens. The youngest among them is about sixteen. Graduates from Farafenni Primary and Middle School, they all attend Farafenni Senior Secondary School where we once taught. You know what they told me last time I was in Farafenni?
"We wish you and Jobe and the others were here to teach us. You were such good teachers."
"Really?" I cried, tears coming to my eyes. "We never knew."
"Yes, you were such good teachers, all of you."
Ahhh Joe, victory! The kids recognized our efforts as builders. As role models. How did they know we were such good teachers? I guess their brothers and sisters whom we taught spread the words. Those folks...our students. The determined ones amongst them are now gainfully employed. In the police force, army, government departments, private companies and so on. I see them often in and around the capital, Banjul, and the commercial towns of Serrekunda and Brikama. I am always so proud of them, especially when they call me:
"Teacher".
It sounds so sweet and soothing in my ears...teacher, that several minutes after departing from them, the name, 'teacher', continues to ring and run around in my brain. We downtrodden teachers. Unsung heroes! Undecorated soldiers! Teachers! They say our reward is in heaven, but somehow, I am reaping my reward here on earth... Some of them even pay my fares in buses and taxis.
"Teacher don't worry?"
"What do you mean Pa Kemo?"
"I've already paid your fare."
"Really?"
"Yes, I've paid."
"Ahhhh, thank you."
Their success is my success, our success, wouldn't you say?

** **

Recall Farafenni, Joe, recall it! Farafenni, that open, flat border town, much

15

hotter than Banjul, especially in the months of March, April and May when we normally took safety jabs against meningitis. Farafenni, that busy town with the muddy smell of the River Gambia. Farafenni, with its assortment of brilliantly plumaged birds and thick-waisted baobab trees, naked of leaves, laden with pendulous, green fruits, inundated with black, brown and red metamorphic rocks, crushable with bare feet. Farafenni holds bittersweet memories for all of us. It was from Farafenni you left: Woke up one morning and said you were tired. You must move on. Can't waste your life teaching. That wasn't what you bargained for when you left Nigeria.

Yes, it wasn't what you bargained for. You bargained for Europe: To make big money.

Me too. What I bargained for when I left Nigeria was not ten years in The Gambia. It wasn't even one year!

And you never told anybody where in Europe you were heading. Only:

"I am off to Europe".

You didn't have enough money to buy a ticket, you never had a visa. Joe...headstrong, that's what you were. How could you have taken such a risk? You could have died! Going to Europe by road. You could have died crossing the great Sahara desert on foot!

You are writing from Malta you say. How did you manage? How did you make it to Malta? Malta! You know, I was always praying for you. Whenever I switched on my short wave radio and listened to the BBC in spite of the terrible static, you came to my mind. All those stories of African migrants drowning in the Mediterranean as rickety boats in which they were travelling capsized; of migrants stranded at the tiny Italian Island of Lampedusa; of migrants being buried alive by sand storms in the Sahara; of migrants being shot at sight by European coast guards as they tried to cross to the 'other side of the river', where the grass seemed greener, in order to make fortunes for themselves and their families!

I thank God and praise Him that you reached your Europe safe and sound, hale and hearty.

** **

Ahhh, the ever-changing Gambian weather. You won't believe it, but now the sun has receded, like the waters of the River Gambia at low tide. A stranger would never believe it almost roasted Banjulians two hours or so ago. And it has left behind a fine, gentle breeze, now blowing lightly, caressing my face lovingly and tickling the leaves of baobab and mango, *neem*, coconut and orange trees. The muezzin's shrill invitation for the 5 o'clock evening prayer, with what I think is a megaphone that had known better days has got adults teeming outside. I'll have to lock my windows in a while...the mosquitoes would be stealing in soon. Only just recovered from malaria last week. Did you hear that again...of course not, but it is the waves crashing at the beach, so loud, so clear, like a mighty explosion. I can hear voices outside my window.

** **

My wife and children! I'm married now Joe! Yes, remind me, go on, remind me...that I swore I would never marry a Gambian. But one of those backsides you said you would lay down your life for nailed me at last. I know you are laughing at me now. I can see your face breaking out in deep creases. I can hear your voice ringing out like a virgin gong. Yes, have fun at my expense, but I'll tell you something: I've learnt one or two things since I sojourned here in The Gambia. One of them is: 'Never say never'. Yes, 'Never ever say never'.

She is very, very pretty and sweet. Brilliant too! She has agreed to follow me to Nigeria and you'll meet her someday. And I've three lovely kids too. Ahhh, you are saying that I may never be able to get to Europe now that I'm married, now that I've responsibilities. No, you are wrong, Joe, you are very wrong. I'll make it to Europe. I have that hunger still, that will! And where there is a will, there is a way. I know this to be true. I'll make it to Europe, and in style. Joe, in style! You want to bet? Don't forget, you've never won a bet with me.

Let me ask you, how old are we now, eh, how old? Nearly forty? Early forty? ...Yes, somewhere there! Joe, do you know that most of our countrymen out here have refused to marry?

"We want to make it before thinking of getting married," they say. "We want to get married ONLY after we've come back from Europe with big bucks."

But what if they never make it to Europe? What if they never make the big bucks they dream of? What if...By the time they realise their mistakes and start 'thinking' of getting married, they would be chasing what, fifty, maybe sixty who knows. Tell me, are you married in Malta?

What really are you doing in Malta? I mean, what kind of job are you doing there? Yes, I know you are a qualified Mechanical Engineer, but are you practicing your profession? Or are you on the streets? I hear guys make it more on the streets doing such things as credit card, advanced fee, mobile cards, drugs, and what have you. You have never been one for the

17

streets, Joe. Oh, you always tried to prove that you were street wise, but you and I know the truth. If there is one thing you are, it is not street wise. So how come you were able to send me such expensive mobile phones and CD players and a brand new laptop computer (with which I'm writing this letter), complete with accessories? Your letter didn't mention your source of livelihood. I'm anxious to know. Please tell me.

Joe, I know that you've a very large heart, but if you are doing what I think you are doing, then think deeply again. You are not doing it for us - your friends and relatives back in Africa - whom you think are stranded, for we are not THAT stranded, really. Let me tell you a story about a new friend I made after you had gone off on your trek.

One day, this new friend got this well crafted letter from his mother. This letter was oozing pain. It dripped agony. This letter asked my friend a lot of difficult questions: Was he cursed? Was he tied to The Gambia? How they were suffering in Nigeria and he was in The Gambia doing nothing, absolutely nothing about it. How his father was sick and she, his mother, could hardly walk and was almost going blind from cataract. How his only brother and sister were dying of starvation. Heartbroken from his family's troubles, this my new friend cried:

"I must change the situation back home...by hook or by crook."

You should have seen him after reading this hot masterpiece. A tall smiling fellow, now he scowled and was doubly bent as if, like Atlas, the troubles of the whole world were squarely dumped on his frail shoulders. A heavy drapery of grief was now wrapped tightly round him, like a wet rag, so much so that with his aquiline nose, he looked like a drenched vulture if you mentally shaved his head clean. And like you, he set out for Europe by foot. He was lucky. He got to Europe. To Germany to be specific.

He must change his family's lot.

At first, he did a little of credit cards. And then, he did a little of mobile phone cards. But these routes were too slow. The dry winds from Africa carried renewed complaints from his family to him all the way to Germany: "...You are not sending enough money home, your mates are already moulding blocks, building skyscrapers, buying big cars. You must send more money if you are not to make yourself and us, your family, a laughing stock."

And so this my friend changed to a faster lane: DRUGS!

And then one day, the anti-drug squad nabbed him. He got ten years for drug trafficking. Do you get the gist now? Don't say you were trying to help us your friends and relatives back home live a better life and then get yourself in trouble.

i remember Syl

(ii)

How is the international airport in Malta? I hope it hasn't been relocated from that open space, surrounded with wicked-looking barbed wire? I can, even now, visualize all those domes and minarets. The beauty of that sprawling little city from the air ...quite unlike the confusion one sees of our Lagos from the air.

How did I know about Malta, you are thinking. I never did tell you I was in Europe, that I was in Malta, did I? No, I didn't hide it from you. The truth is that the discussion never came up among the millions of discussions we had under the sometimes cloudy, but mostly clear starry sky of Farafenni nights; or as, holding hands, we strolled side by side in the cool evenings, enjoying the landscape of Farafenni and licking the sweet, smooth, fluffy whiteness off seeds of baobab fruits, or enjoying the deep sour, but irresistible tang as we bit into the fleshy bodies of Saloum plums, yellow but mostly green; or as we ate Ngburu Nyembe during school recesses when we sheltered from the fierce sun in the staff room, or hid under huge, and full-foliaged mango trees, as we took a break from the noisy students we taught.

Yes, I was in Europe.

** **

After graduating in Economics from the University of Calabar, like millions of graduates, I made my way to that hubbub of a city, Lagos, in search of a nice paying job. I expected to go with my job, a car, and a well-furnished apartment in one of Lagos's exclusive neighbourhoods. After all, was I not a graduate? And was my country, our country, Nigeria, not endowed with so much oil wealth?

Five years, Joe. Five years of wandering up and down Lagos like a fugitive ...like a derelict; years of hunger, of near starvation, living in run-down tenement buildings, under bridges; five whole years of shame and I was ready to do anything, anything. Psychologically I was defeated. Mentally I was drained. Physically I was subdued.

My neck, like a vulture's, stuck out of blanched and faded t-shirts. My trousers had gaping holes by my crotch, and like a female, I had to be conscious of how I sat. You should have seen my singlets, torn everywhere, like a lunatic's. My toes and heels peeked out of my socks, and the soles of my only shoes were so 'chopped' that as I sauntered along, I felt the stones on my bare feet, sharp and uncompromisingly hot or cold, depending on the frame of mind of Lagos's moody weather. Every office I went to, the sign " No Vacancies", winked wickedly at me! And as I turned my back and walked dejectedly away, I thought I heard the sign "No Vacancies", double over in rib-racking raucous laughter. I was going mad. But I was frugal. I was always a frugal person. All the money classmates who had poured into advanced fee frauds (419) and other illegal deals dashed me, and the few naira I earned doing odd jobs, I had saved, never expending a dime on an ordinary bottle of Coke or iced water. Then I put out the words: I wanted out. Out of Nigeria, and fast. I was simply fed up with the system. With everything! Some understanding guys got me a visa for Poland.

"You'll enter Poland, and our pals in Germany will come rescue you and take you across the border to Germany," the guys who issued me the Polish visa assured. Apart from the huge visa fee, nearly US$2,500.00, I also paid them about US$500.00 for the extra favour of getting their pals to smuggle me into Germany.

"I'll make it in Europe," I told myself. "Big bucks."

No direct flight to Warsaw, and I had to obtain a transit visa for Moscow, this time all by myself. Somehow, those understanding guys could not help me with a transit visa. They were suddenly too busy. My journey was delayed for a month, but finally, I had my transit visa. And I also met these two guys, Abel and Lawson. We were on a similar mission...going to Europe where the grass was greener. Abel and Lawson were as alike as two peas from the same pod. Now that I think of it, I think they were related. Tall, lanky, fair skinned fellows. They bleached their skins to look light, what with the offensive odours of dead skin they oozed. Half of the time we were together, I was either struggling to avoid spitting, or had my breath suspended at intervals!

I didn't have more than US$150.00 on me, having spent my Basic Travelling Allowance (BTA) for the transit visa, which I hadn't bargained for. Abel and Lawson had all the money, US dollars in tiny one-dollar bills. They had bundles of them, nearing one thousand apiece. But they couldn't read. In fact, identifying their names was a problem, and they had to tell their passports apart by flipping quickly to the picture page! And as for writing, forget it. What were they going to Europe to do without any education, I wondered.

But it wasn't my business, was it? If I, a graduate went through all those pains looking for a job and couldn't get any, imagine the plight of an illiterate. And mind you, illiterates or not, they had the same aspirations as you and I: a good life comprising of a nice house, a car, wife, lots of kids, plenty to eat and drink, good businesses and lots of nice things for younger folks and parents and relatives back in the village. So it was a symbiotic association Abel, Lawson and I had: I'll read the road signs and point out the way when we got to Europe. In return, they will be free with their dollars. Perfect arrangement, wouldn't you say?

** **

You know what, Joe, my wife is preparing dinner. It will be benachin. I can smell the meat and onions frying ...uuummmm ...aahhh, and I can smell garlic too...my kids are happy, they love benachin. I can hear them singing their nursery rhymes.

...Ahhhh, family life is so interesting. Though, I tell you, it is not all sugar. One has to work at it. Did I tell you my wife's name? Haddy. Haddy Mbye! My Haddy is a Wolof. Nangadef Joe...how are you, Joe? I now speak more of Wolof, and have forgotten nearly all the Mandinkas we used to twist our tongues around while at Farafenni. Unlike most Wolofs, she is fair skinned, a touch of Narr (Arab) blood, she explained to me while we were courting. She is of average height and has these slight bandy legs that make her so sexy especially when she has on tight jeans, which she favours. Round, clear brown eyes, and her voice, tingling, always arousing my tendon, hardening it...

You know, I followed Haddy to the Mosque, to wed her, amidst the judgmental glares of our friends. From the beginning, my former Church elders at the 'Life Given Bread Church' saw my Haddy as nothing but a 'Jezebel', and the accursed 'Serpent' himself.

"She has given him 'something' to eat," they cried, their eyes blazing.

And they took it upon themselves, declaring a seven days dry fasting to 'exorcise' and 'cast' her out of my system using scriptural injunctions.

But like superglue, my love for her held!

So my dear, what I'm trying to tell you in essence now is that five times a day, I go down facing east; five times a day, I go down facing Mecca.

I'm now a Muslim!

Shaving off my soft, woolly hair, the Imams at my Mosque re-baptized and gave me a new name: 'Tapha', short for 'Mustapha'.

My family's outright rejection didn't anger, worry, or frighten me. Love... Oh love... It can face all things! Though sometimes... sometimes... Ahhh, sometimes...

Joe, tell me, Islam and Christianity, aren't they both about one God?

21

Aren't they both about one Sovereign Being? Why do we keep battering ourselves for nothing? You are disappointed, like the rest of them, aren't you? Despite the distance between us, I can see the disgust in your face. Look, just take me as I am. PLEASE, don't stop liking me. Don't despise me simply because I worship God in a different way now.

** **

Eventually, Abel, Lawson and I were airborne, on our way to Europe and to wealth. We departed around noon one fine day and touched down at the Sheremetyevo international airport in Moscow the next day.

The first thing that struck me about Europe was the freezing cold! And to imagine that the sun was shining, almost ablaze in the clear sky, though there was this hazy halo surrounding it! In a hurry to flee Nigeria, we had forgotten to take along thick clothing. Our ears froze in no time. Brittle and easily breakable, it ached like hell. As we spoke to each other, we saw our breaths condensing in front of our very noses.

We had transit visas and had no problems entering the city. We rode an electric train, the first time I had ridden in one. The thing malfunctioned, and kept jerking and jerking, embarrassing me. (You know, I never believed anything European could malfunction!) Soon, we were in a hotel room. It wasn't particularly what we expected a European hotel room to look like. But then, between the three of us, we didn't pay much for it, only about US $150, cheap by Moscow standards we were told by the hotel receptionist, a flabby old lady.

Then we went out to take a peek around town. We saw the Kremlin. Abel and Lawson commented on how it was simply an ancient building of old stones towering to the sky. And having heard so much about the KGB, they were adamant we kept a safe distance. I tried to explain that tourists were always crawling all over the place snapping pictures, and pointed to a group of middle-aged Chinese men and women with cameras hanging from their necks, but they wouldn't budge.

So I sought out and read aloud a few more signboards, and we changed course. This time to the Patrice Lumumba University. When we got there, Abel and Lawson swore we were in a secondary school premises. I was speechless myself. Patrice Lumumba was a disappointment. It didn't compare to a third rate university back home! Then we saw these Russian lads. They were haggard looking fellows with clean-shaven heads. Their jean trousers were slashed at the knees and laps. Their blue eyes flashed. Excitedly, they approached us, each running his tongue tentatively over his lower lip:

"Do you guys have any for sale?" they chorused, jostling each other for a better view.

"Any what? What are they talking about?" Abel and Lawson whispered. I shivered.

"Heroin, Coke, crack."

"We are not here for that," I said. .

"We will give you good price. We know you guys have it, you always do."

We rushed back to the safety of our hotel room, panting like dying Labrador dogs. The cold, Christ! It must have been below zero! Later we did something we should have done a long time before: Huddled together to keep warm, we took a closer look at our Polish visas and to our dismay, discovered huge dissimilarities. Even to Abel and Lawson, the differences were clearly obvious. We bowed our heads and thought our private thoughts. Several painful minutes dragged by.

"We would have to cross into Poland by road," I advised. "Warsaw by air would be too tight."

It was nearly a two-day train ride to the Russian border with Poland. And then disaster struck!

"Your visas say Warsaw," said the Russian immigration officer at their end of the border. "Yes, we know," I replied, with heart pounding. "We are tourists. We want to see the Polish countryside."

"You must go back. You can't go this way."

"But they can, why not?"

Five Polish youths, no more than eighteen years each rushed miraculously to our rescue. They loved Black Americans, we looked like Black Americans. Were we Black Americans? Nigerians? They had never heard of Nigeria. Anyway, it didn't matter. They took the matter upon themselves to the chagrin of the Russian immigration officers.

"We go to our immigration office over there," the fine lads told us, pointing. "There, you get stamp, no problem. These fools are ignorant. America good country, we like America."

The Russians abused the Polish youths with an onslaught of profanity, calling them traitors. The youths didn't mind, damn good folks. The youths explained everything to their immigration officers at their end of the border. The officers were sympathetic. They were so sorry. Immigration procedures were stringent. Had the visas read land, they would have given us immediate access. If we still wanted to come in by land, no problems, but could we go back to Moscow and get new visas. The Polish Embassy in Moscow would issue them without delay. Our Polish friends were very sorry to see their 'American' friends turned back. We swapped addresses.

"When we reach Warsaw, we will look you guys up," I assured them,

23

disappointment written all over my face.

"Very, very good, thank you," they chorused. Abel and Lawson, who for the most part had been quiet, smiled. I had no time for such luxury. The reason was simple: I had no money for the return journey.

"What happened to all your money?" Lawson exploded at the ticketing office when I spread out the contents of my wallet on the cashier's counter, looking for money I knew was not there. He and Abel had bought me the one-way ticket out of Moscow. "We can't continue to carry you on our backs," he warned further.

"I know," I said.

"Look, Mister, our money is fast going," Abel pointed out.

"I know," I replied.

"We will have to go our separate ways," Lawson threatened.

I played my trump card:

"Who will read out the road signs to you guys?"

"We will manage," they said.

But they bought me the return train ticket.

Two days later, at Sheremetyevo, we boarded the plane headed for Warsaw. We feared the worst and shook like leaves rattled by angry wind as the plane wrestled with mountains of cumulous cloud.

Once in Warsaw, we saw war!

One peek at our visas and we were sequestered, all three of us. Our light green passports further compounded our dilemma. Three black folks among a multitude of Europeans, Asians, Americans and other 'sweet-smelling' nationalities. An obese immigration officer soon confiscated our passports, disappearing with them into an inner office with a glass door. You should have seen the disdain on her red, bloated face. She wore it like a prized mask. 'Sweet-smelling' white, red and yellow faces glared at us. What cheek! We simply glared back! They whispered in foreign tongues. My imagination rioted with interpretations:

Drugs!

Always drugs!

Africans!

"Your visas are not in order," the immigration officer came out to announce, having concluded a series of 'hush-hush' talk with a superior and listening long on a red telephone. Craning my neck, I had watched her every move through the glass door.

"What is not in order about it?" I wanted to know, feigning anger.

"Forged! We just spoke to Lagos."

ANNULOWANO was soon stamped on the visas, annulling them, and by association our passports. We were shown the way back to the plane.

Our feet had not even touched the Polish soil. Our repatriation back to Africa had begun.

(iii)

Back in Moscow, I understood why some Nigerians hate to be known as such. I understood why some Nigerians want to throw their Nigerian nationality to the dogs and pigs and acquire the nationality of other -even lesser- countries. The airport authorities detained us, as well as other Nigerian and African deportees. There were Tanzanians, Kenyans, Somalians, Ethiopians, Guineans, Ghanaians, Senegalese and so on. They too had been sent back to await a plane back to Africa. Like my two friends and I, many others were being sent back to Africa because of faked visas. But many, many others were being sent back, especially Nigerians, for frivolous and untenable reasons. The Guineans and Senegalese and Tanzanians called their ambassadors, and help came quickly. Their cases were sorted out and they were once more on their way, to a better future. The Kenyans, Somalians and Ethiopians did the same, and help came quickly.

"Why can't we call the Nigerian embassy here in Moscow," someone suggested. "They should come and help us."

Someone dug out the number and rang the Nigerian Embassy as we all gathered, listening and hoping for help from the Giant of Africa. Over the speakerphone:

"Please can I...we speak to the Ambassador..."

"I ..we ...who ...who exactly are..."

"We're Nigerians stranded here at the Sheremetyevo airport in Moscow."

And the line went dead, dead cold!

They should have at least listened to us, to our tales. For Christ's sake, they should have at least heard us out. Simple courtesy! If after listening to us, they decided none of us- the entire lot of ten Nigerians- needed help of any sort, then so be it. We would have borne them no grudge, not a tiny bit of rancour. But no, they treated us like rabid dogs, poisons to be kept at bay.

And so we spent over a week at the airport, sleeping on the hard, freezing bare floor. Eating what one of us could buy and share with the others. Thank God I had learnt to fast when I worshipped with one Pentecostal Church in Yaba, Lagos, whose pastor promised jobs, healings, successes and riches upon completion of his prescribed stringent fasting regimen. (Don't laugh, please, for this is not a laughing matter). Else I would

25

have died of starvation.

On a more serious note, the way we were treated by our embassy, the representative of our elected government in Russia shocked me to my bones. We were like dog dung! The least I had expected was some level of responsibility and concern, seeing how far away we were from home. But then, home or abroad, a skunk would stink.

Why? Why bother call yourself a Nigerian when the Nigerian government would do nothing for you? Why? Why bother call yourself a Nigerian when the Nigerian government doesn't care about you, whether you lived or died.

It was after this rotten, shameful, degrading and left-handed treatment that I decided to rethink my identity. Yes, rethink my nationality.

The returning Boeing 747 had made a stop to refuel. We were allowed to stretch our legs. I didn't have a watch, but it wasn't 9:00 a.m.

"Why should I go back to Nigeria?" I asked myself as I trudged down the aeroplane's ladder. "To continue struggling day after day without a job? To further add to the hordes of jobless and idle youths who flood the nation?"

I didn't want to join the numerous other young, vile graduates who had delved into the fast lane of advanced fee frauds and blood money from ritual killings. I knew I didn't have what it took to survive. I wanted to work for my money. I knew there was dignity in labour, but I was being frustrated.

"What was in Nigeria for me except more pain and suffering?" I wondered. "I must do something. I must not allow myself to be deported back to Lagos to wallow in abject poverty."

That was how I sneaked inside a toilet and firmly locked the door. An hour later, I breathed a sigh of relief as, through the windows, I saw the plane airborne. Finally, its wispy white, exhaust smoke and the metallic, deafening sound of its Rolls-Royce engines disappeared with it into the clear blue sky.

Gingerly unlocking the toilet door, I strode out to the noisy arrival lounge. To my dismay I discovered that the airport was in the middle of nowhere. The only way out was a ride along the motorway. There was no place to hide, no trees or shrubs. I spied in the distance barbed wire fences surrounding the airport. Rooted firmly to the ground in confusion, I was thinking of what step to take, when to my chagrin, I saw and recognized the plane that had taken off only a moment ago as it taxied to a stop on the smooth asphalt tarmac. Uprooting myself, my legs came instantly alive and quickly, I dashed back to my toilet sanctuary. From there, I listened to the hullabaloo rippling through the lounge.

"A male passenger is missing," a woman screamed. "He must still be around, we have not been gone for more than ten minutes."

The authorities searched the toilets and other places where a person could possibly conceal himself.

"This toilet is locked," a man called out, a soldier probably, what with his gruffy voice.

The door's handle was tried again and again. Someone placed his shoulder against the door and heaved. It held! Soon a crowd gathered, excited voices, in various languages ranging from English to Arabic, rose and fell as the airport authorities tried to find the door's spare key.

"Open up," the gruffy voice called out. "Passenger number 18, we know you are there. We have seen you from the camera."

I looked around and a tiny camera sunk into the wall peeked at me from a far corner. I tried to swallow but my parched throat wouldn't let me.

"I'm not going back to Nigeria," I croaked.

"Open up, please."

"Sanni Abacha is after me, he is after my life. He'll kill me."

"The game is up. Open up now, we have seen you."

After several minutes of dilly-dallying, I opened up. Several soldiers smiled at me wickedly. I almost laughed out (loud) when I mentally compared their automatic rifles with the rusted, comic looking German G-3 and Russian AK-47 rifles our ill-fed soldiers brandished and threatened locals with at roadblocks and checkpoints. But this was no time for laughter. Instead, I cried:

"Abacha will kill me. I demand my human rights. I'm not going back to Lagos."

"We are not going to Lagos. This plane is bound for Cotonou, Benin Republic," an obviously relieved airhostess assured me.

"Cotonou? Only a stone throw from Lagos. It's the same thing. He is looking for me everywhere. He has eyes everywhere."

Three mean-looking soldiers hung their automatics on their backs, broad as barns and began rolling up their sleeves. Thick biceps, like giant yam mounds confronted me. They were determined to carry me in at all costs. I deeply enjoyed the consternation written all over their faces as suddenly, I began marching towards the plane. Later that day, nearing midnight, the plane taxied to a stop at the International airport in Cotonou.

I didn't cross the border into Nigeria. Why should I? I wasn't stupid. Why should I when I had heard fantastic stories about a certain place ...a certain small tourist country called The Gambia, further along the west coast?

** **

The fact, as you must have gleaned from the above narration is that for me, The Gambia wasn't planned. It was simply an escape valve for my frustrated European journey. I meant to come here, work for a few months, and then proceed to Europe again, to make my big bucks. But ten years on, ten whole years on my dear friend, I'm still here, merely peddling chalk. CHALK! CHALK!

But be that as it may, I'm still determined to go to Europe. I've no choice in the matter, really. I have to better my lot. I have to better the lot of my immediate and extended families. Europe is the place. Unless, unless something dramatically positive happens to our country, Nigeria. And I don't see that happening in the near future, not with the way our 'born-again' president is running our country.

I remember when I was about to leave the university. The day I wrote my final exams, I had blunted my pen and sworn I would never write another exam. And the day I walked out of the university gate with my Bachelor's degree under my armpit, I had sworn never to set foot in any other university campus for the purpose of study. Nearly twenty years on and I terribly regret all those vows, vows made out of what should I say now, youthful exuberance. How I now wish to go back to a university. How I wish to write an exam now, any exam that would today land me in a European university! I desperately need my Masters degree. And my doctorate too. I want to go to Europe to study. Academics, that is where the magic for a good quality life lies …at least for me; making big bucks is no longer the incentive, the attraction for going to Europe. Big bucks doesn't necessarily translate to a good life, but of course you would argue that obtaining a PhD doesn't either. But that is what I want. Europe for academics, for self-emancipation, NOT for big bucks! Big bucks have never meant emancipation! Ask me and I will tell you (But that is another story).

You once said that once you set foot out of The Gambia, you would never return. Do you still feel the same? About The Gambia …about not coming back? I don't think The Gambia is what we used to think it was. Agreed, it is a small country, but it isn't useless. It isn't retrogressive either. You may say I feel differently because I am now married to a Gambian and have Gambian relatives, but I say that is not why. I see things a bit differently. Clearer so to speak, not with that same eye with which we saw things in the early nineties when we first arrived as hustlers.

I think you have changed too. I was rather shocked to receive your letter, not to talk of the beautiful gifts you sent me. Giving gifts was never

28

your strong point. You made this clear in Farafenni when your numerous girlfriends complained you never sent them anything, not even on 'Valentine's Day'. Do you remember? The tone of your letter made it quite clear.

But I tell you one thing, you are lucky to have left when you did. Everything changed that academic year you left. We became slaves, more or less and were worked to our very bones.

"They'll work for even longer hours," the school authorities said, even to our hearing. "They would be jobless if they went back to their country." We said nothing. There was nothing to say!

And the economy became bad. The dalasi devalued by more than 300 percent. Who else to bear the blame for the worsening economy, but foreigners? And which foreigners? Nigerians! You won't believe it, but our residential permit is no longer D500 but D1, 300. And a new tax, 'Alien Tax' was introduced. Every Nigerian pays D1, 000. Nigerians can no longer drive taxis here. Taxation for those who own businesses has skyrocketed. And there is talk in the air that next year, things would be doubly difficult!

Why don't we go back home, you are asking? Home to where? Nigeria? To confront all the religious riots? To confront the Northern Talibans? To confront the carnage in the Delta region? You've forgotten where I come from: East, since abandoned by the federal government in terms of developmental projects.

And from where will I get a new job? With which money will I pay a five-year house rent, what with Shylocks for landlords? You see why going home will be difficult? You see why going home is difficult? You see why I've to move forward, to Europe? Even if it is doing as you did: walking all the way, through the great Sahara desert, swimming the Mediterranean and braving the sniper's bullet at Lampedusa!

Joe, the saddest thing is that to be called a Nigerian out here in The Gambia now is a heavy cross to bear. I know it's the same in Europe, I was there, remember, and have never forgotten the manner in which that female Polish immigration officer handled our green passports, genteelly, as if they were crawling with the Ebola and AIDS virus, or had excrement smeared over them. That particular experience continues to torture me.

There is so much anti-Nigerian sentiment out there. Why do other nationalities abhor us so, why? This negative attitude is driving innocent Nigerians insane. It's driving me bananas. Other nationalities take one look, just one look at us and are threatened. Threatened of what, I don't know. Only if they know what you and I know, that deep within, the average Nigerian harbours deep fears …that it is the fear of this fear that makes him appear fearless, just so as to prevent himself from buckling under.

I think it is this seeming fearlessness in our demeanour that people detest. I think it is based on this seeming fearlessness in our carriage that makes people antagonize us with all their hearts, and with all their might! Everyday that passes, I see Nigerians gradually becoming like the Jews as is written down in history! Hated by all. Loved by none!

And it isn't as if the Nigerian authorities, our government, aren't aware of these anti-Nigerian sentiments, these gross injustices meted out on her citizens. They are, for God's sake. But what do they do, those we have elected to protect us, what do they do? Sit and do nothing. Absolutely *nothing*. I've never heard of the Nigerian government lodging a complaint against another country for the maltreatment of her citizens. Other countries do it from time to time.

But instead what do we get? What?

Nigerian government sending out our soldiers on peacekeeping missions. To go and die for nothing. To die for countries that would never appreciate our innocent blood spilled.

How many Nigerian soldiers died for nothing fighting Charles Taylor in Liberia? How did the Nigerian government show its concern for these dead soldiers? How?

By giving Charles Taylor asylum in our own Nigeria!

How many Nigerians did Charles Taylor amputate? How did the Nigerian government show its disgust?

By giving Charles Taylor a presidential mansion in Calabar, providing him round the clock military guard and ensuring that he and his family go to bed with their tummies filled to the brim.

With whose money, eh, with whose money are these feats being accomplished?

Our money, our taxpayers' money of course, while the average taxpayer and his family go to bed hungry, with stomachs growling in protest.

How many Nigerians do you think died trying to bring peace to Sierra Leone? And now poor Nigerian troops are trooping to far away Western Darfur in Sudan, to go and die.

Of course, we must prove we are the Giant of Africa!

WHAT BULLSHIT!

And what does the average Nigerian get in return for these humanitarian assistances rendered by our 'sorry heart' government, what? Ridicule. Molestation. Imprisonment. Haranguing. Death. Yes, even death!

**   **

(iv)

My dear Joe,

I ask you again: Do you remember Syl? Yes, Syl! Do you still remember him? You gave him his nickname, 'One Side', because he walked like a crab...side, side, side, a case of mild polio in his childhood.

By the time you arrived in Farafenni, we were already there, Syl and I and the others...Akin, Clive, Ola, Josh, Chris. Syl was one of the first Nigerians in Farafenni. I knew him the best, so let me tell you more about him.

Did you know he had a first class in Animal Science from the University of Nigeria, Nsukka? Oh yes, he did. Syl was among one of the most brilliant people I ever knew. As you can attest, he had such a vast knowledge that he could discuss any topic under the sun, from astrology to zoology. That explains why his voice was loudest those nights we spent arguing and shouting at the top of our voices after our dinners of the wood-like Fula bread, *tapalapa,* and bowls of scalding tea.

Syl wanted to set up and own the biggest poultry and pig farm you ever saw. He had graduated in 1980 -just when you and I were entering university. Try, as he could to secure a bank loan to start off, he failed.

"Collateral," the banks snarled at him.

He tried to explain that he was an only son, just out of the university, father dead, relatives poor. But the banks didn't care. They laughed and shooed him out of their exotic premises. He approached one influential person after another in his hometown. There were so sorry, they told him. They didn't want to invest in poultry. And they didn't like pigs. Pigs were dirty!

But Syl was made of steel.

"I must succeed," he swore. "I must make it."

And then he heard those tales you and I had heard: about The Gambia. About the places in The Gambia called 'German', and 'London Corner', where you could get a bus ride to Germany and Britain respectively. And like us, he picked out the Atlas and sought out The Gambia. He learnt it was a small country of only about 1.2 million. No natural resources. Subsistence agriculture the main stay of the economy. Seasonal tourism. Illiteracy rate, highest in the West African sub-region. Only two major hospitals! And yet he took off, what with the heady tales of this 'German', and 'London Corner'.

Sometimes, I wonder who gave life to these deadly tales. And then, like a very contagious disease, it spread so fast that every Adamu, Agu and

Akande in Nigeria who could afford the transport cost was in a hurry to get to this 'London Corner', and 'German'. Some even stole money, while others sold their parent's landed properties. One thing Syl never told anyone was that he was hypertensive. It was embarrassing to him, to have been diagnosed of such a disease. I found out by chance, and was shocked. He swore me to secrecy. He told me:
"Can you believe it, I was diagnosed in my mid twenties."
I didn't know what to say, and I couldn't say, 'sorry'. Syl didn't like to be told sorry, remember? Said it made him feel funny. And because he felt embarrassed at his hypertension, he refused treatment!

Whenever he had cause to go to the hospital, he was given a load of Nifedipine and other anti-hypertensives. But no sooner had he left the hospital premises than, *fiam*, he flung them far, far into the bush. That was something I found strange about Syl. With all his intelligence...a sound and solid first class in Animal Science! Who else should have known about the idiosyncrasies of the human body? Who else should have known that the human body was nothing more than a simple, but highly glorified machine...that it could fail and fall, like our milk teeth, without a moment's notice? Syl knew and lectured us about such concepts as the human genome, quantum and particle physics and other scientific abracadabra...and yet...

By the time he arrived in The Gambia, he was actually quite ill. He was probably devastated with all the negatives he received while questing for a bank loan to kick-start his poultry and pig farms.

"I believed so much in the system," he told me. "I never believed any one in his right thinking mind would turn down my request for a loan, especially when I had made such a wonderful grade in school."

That was the impression, the promise his professors at Nsukka had given him, and that was why, he told me, he had read so hard, shunning goodtime and rest, and burnt the midnight candle on both ends, given that his father was dead, had died poor, and he had no 'Abraham' for a godfather. Doing well in school, he strongly believed, was his only chance to success!

How wrong everything...his beliefs, his professors' promises turned out to be. He thought about that poultry and pig farm morning, afternoon and night. He literarily lived for it, that poultry and pig farm. As you can attest to, he neither drank, nor smoked, and had no sin, except that once in a while, he...he masturbated in his hands, using his toilet soap (how many times did I catch him at that?), but then, no man is without a vice. Even me, I had and still have my own small faults...what...what with my visiting the prostitutes every once in a while.

**   **

In fact, you've to thank Jesus for me. Since I married, I've been with them, I mean the prostitutes, how many times now, let me see …one, two, three, four, five, yes, only five times since the last seven years. It used to be so regular then, when we were in Farafenni, remember? And this HIV/AIDS scare, God, is it real (you know I've this morbid fear of catching some terrible disease)?…I've promised myself severally to call it quits…anyway, I'm trying…and to imagine that my wife, Haddy is so pretty. Joe, these prostitutes, they keep attracting me like a magnet attracts iron fillings; like a corpse attract flies …do you think I should see a psychiatrist? Anyway, I always use a condom, what do you think? I don't want to pass anything to my Haddy!

**   **

Anyway, five years ago, Syl went home. You'd already trekked off to Europe. Syl went home and came back a broken man. Really broken. And full of regrets. They'd all made it, he told me. Most of his friends, class and age mates had made it. Big cars, fine houses, beautiful wives, wonderful children. By now, he would at least have gotten married, had children, he loved children. He shouldn't have left.

"But why didn't you remain then?" I asked.

"Baaaa…." He cried. "Remain? Remain to do what? Remain and be mocked by folks I was better than in school?"

And so Syl worked extra hard in the school. He was determined to go to Europe, at all cost, come what may. And then he talked about you. Day and night, he whimpered about you. You became his hero.

"Joe is brave," he would cry.

I would say nothing.

"Joe is very brave. At the end of this academic year, not a day later."

And not only did he teach Agric Science, his specialty, he now brought his extra knowledge to bear. He taught Math, Biology and even stood in for the English teacher, for two terms!

"I need the extra money for the end of this academic year to be a reality," he told me.

You should have seen him. He now limped more, walking more and more like a crab, side, side, side …you would think he was approaching you but he was rather ambling away at a curious angle.

"My poultry and pig farm must be a reality," he told me, so much so that in my sleep, all I heard was Syl's grinding moan: 'My poultry and pig farm must be a reality.'

And Syl forgot that age was telling on him, he was almost forty-five. Worst of all, he neglected his high blood pressure: "My BP is normal," he would repeat again and again. Most local teachers had deserted the provinces. The salary was too meagre, they said. That was how come Syl could teach more than one subject as well as stand in for the English teacher. The school authorities praised him: how he was the ideal teacher, and was desirable, how others like me whom they had had so much hope in had terribly disappointed them. And the more they sang his praises, the more Syl slaved.

Then, one evening, as he made an 'Osmosis' demonstration in the Biology practical class, he had a blackout! He had actually been complaining of this severe headache. Didn't he think it was due to his high BP? No, it was the severe Farafenni weather, the unbearably high temperature. Why not go to the hospital, just to make sure? Oh Boy, don't talk about my pressure! 'Boy', remember? That was what he always called me.

It was indeed a fatal stroke. He was rushed to the Farafenni Health Centre. That night, the nurse on duty broke the sad news that Syl was paralysed on one side. I noted it was on his one good side. That same night, his condition deteriorated and he slipped into a coma.

"We will have to move him," the nurse announced the next day.

"In this condition?" I asked, shocked.

"We don't have the facilities to sustain his life in this comatose state," she revealed.

First it was to Bansang Hospital, and finally to the Royal Victoria Teaching Hospital in Banjul. Try as they could, the Cuban doctors couldn't revive him. The last time he uttered one intelligible word was as he was rushed to the Farafenni Health Centre. He simply croaked in my ears: 'My poultry and pig farm.'

And then one morning, I went to see him. His bed was empty. Only a mattress, stripped of its blanket stared at me. Seeing my confusion, a nurse approached me.

"Where is the patient occupying this bed...this bed here?" I stammered.

"The one that was brought a week ago?"

"Yes."

"That stroke patient?"

"Yes, that stroke patient."

"Oh, he died...around 5 O'clock this morning."

Cold sweat broke out all over my body and with mouth wide open, I inhaled a sizeable dose of disinfectants.

"Check the mortuary," the nurse advised me. "It is just by the white building over there," she said pointing.

At the mortuary, I watched Syl being washed, in preparation for refrigeration. The preservative, formalin, was being pumped into his body through his collapsed vessels. I searched for signs that would tell me it was all a lie, a big lie, that Syl wasn't dead, that he was still alive. But his hairy chest was steady in death, not heaving. His complexion was a deathly parlour, his skin having been drained of life. I beheld his broad flat nose, and recalled how it often flared, firing warm air as he took up any one who wished to argue on the 'Politics of Oil', or 'Rogue Nations', or 'The Decadence of the Nigerian Ruling Class.' I beheld his face, with subtle growth of days old beard, which would grow no more. It was contorted with, I think, pain. Or, regret. Or, humiliation. Or, embarrassment. Or, all!

You know what, I didn't cry. No, I didn't cry for Syl. For one, he wouldn't have sanctioned it, my crying for him. But that wasn't why I didn't cry. I didn't cry for the simple reason that Syl had lost nothing in death. To me, he had only transcended. He had only transited to another plane, a higher plane. He had simply moved on, perhaps to a place where he would get all the loan he wanted to float his state-of-the-art poultry and pig farms.

But I did shed buckets of tears for our dear country, Nigeria. For by losing someone like Syl, our country had lost something invaluable.

He was one of the most determined, hard working and intelligent fellows I ever saw. What wouldn't he have done to make good in Nigeria, if only he had had half the chance? If only he had gotten a quarter of the encouragement he so desperately sought. Sometimes, I blame the system, our government for his fate and the fate of millions of others like him. I know of him, myself and you, my dear Joe, how we have suffered, and continue suffering amidst plenty, our country's plenty. But there are thousands, no, millions of others out there, scattered around the globe, like chaff in the wind, trying unsuccessfully, yes unsuccessfully, to squeeze water out of stone, eating dust, nothing but victims of chronic mismanagement and mal-administration in our great, rich country, Nigeria, the supposed Pearl of the 'Black Race' and Africa!

Do you feel hot tears sting your eyes? Don't cry, don't. Though I can't help myself, my tears are simply flowing, doing a free fall. Thank God my wife and kids are already asleep. To see a grown man like me crying would have broken their hearts. They have never seen me cry before. But to tell you the truth, even if they did now, I won't mind, not when I'm crying for my broken country, Nigeria.

Did you hear that Chinua Achebe cried for Nigeria only recently? That was when he rejected our country's second largest honour, the 'Commander of the Federal Republic' (CFR) award. Who needs an award hanging uselessly, like a withered appendage, when two thirds of his fellow citizens are eating from the refuse dumps? Who needs an award when in his country, one that produces vast quantities of oil, the largest barrels per day in Africa, there is no electricity?

Who needs an award when every other day there is a strike in his country, union leaders pitched against the government who are forever increasing the price of petroleum products, quadrupling the economic burden on the ordinary citizen whose ordeal they are inert to?

Of what use is an award to a man with a conscience when in his country, university lecturers are not appropriately remunerated; when like a chronic haemorrhage, his country is being incapacitated with massive brain drain; when graduates can't find work; when there are no essential medicines in hospitals and clinics?

Of what use is an award to a right-thinking Nigerian when there is environmental degradation in the Niger-Delta, when farms and streams from which the local inhabitants derive their daily sustenance are heavily polluted by oil spillage, when there is no portable water, roads, schools, hospitals in the Delta region, whose oil supports government's uncountable elephant projects in other parts of the country and pays for peace keepers in countries fighting irrelevant wars in which the ruling class do nothing but smile to the banks with the spoils of war?

Tell me, of what use is an award to a God-fearing man when more than 10,000 innocent Nigerians have died during communal clashes since 1999? Why won't Achebe feel betrayed, and broken-hearted like you and I and millions of other Nigerians? To imagine that our government, despite the myriad social problems it has to attend to, still has time for making and presenting awards. It reminds me of that proverb about the foolish man who chases rats while his house burns!

Sorry I digressed, but man, sometimes, I get so pissed off thinking, according to Achebe of the 'dangerous' state of affairs in our Nigeria, 'a country that does not work'.

** **

It was Syl's burial that really broke my heart, shredded it! The shoddiest event I ever saw, a slapdash, an apology...for one so brilliant, one so enterprising, one so determined. A foreign log of wood in a foreign country, that was what his body, his corpse became. No body wanted to take responsibility, not even the school, for whom he was a star, a shining example, and for whom he was toiling while his stroke struck.

He should have been flown home to Nigeria for proper burial, why not? Because suddenly, the school realized something vitally important: There wasn't such a vote, to fly a deceased Nigerian teacher home in the school's financial outlay for that year, or for any other year for that matter. The school said they were sorry, but the truth was the truth: Flying a deceased teacher to his home country for burial was not a priority. And the ministry of education too had no such vote in their yearly budget, to fly home a deceased foreign teacher who had contributed immensely to the development of streams of young Gambians.

But saddest was the Nigerian Embassy. They too had no such vote, to fly a dead compatriot home.

"Ours is a small consulate, a grade D consulate," they said. "We do not have the vote-"

But of course, a small consulate or not, a grade Z or a grade D consulate or not, there was a vote, plenty of votes to buy four wheel drives in their numbers, pick up prostitutes, keep concubines, live in mansions and travel overseas for headaches, toothaches, boils and minor itches in the buttocks and armpits...as well as for the wives of tenth grade diplomats to have their babies overseas!

And so Syl, our dear Syl was buried in a shallow grave in the Banjul cemetery, near the sea, the roaring Atlantic Ocean. The grave is presently unmarked! Last time I was there, I almost missed it, nearly stood on it. When we committed him to mother earth, we had erected for him a simple epitaph, which read:

'Here lies the remains of Sylvester Chukwumma, a Nigerian teacher. Died May 2000.'

The epitaph has since been blown away by the elements. You know, like you, Syl and I were very close, especially so when you went off on your trek, and I had no one else to dream with. So now, at the slightest opportunity, I visit his *gravesite*, just to say hi. Even when I drive past the cemetery in public *transports*, I find a moment to wave to him, using my mind's hand. I'll never forget him: His enthusiasm, diligence, determination, intelligence and his death.

Yes I'll never forget his death!

I think I owe him a favour. A duty I believe I owe myself too. Someday when I might have gone to Europe and acquired all the education I want, with the financial benefits I know will accrue with it, I'll come back to The Gambia. I'll never forget The Gambia ...for Syl! You know, he is not happy. And I'm not hallucinating when I say this. He has told me, in my dreams.

"I want to go HOME," he says.
I've given him my word. Someday I'll come back to The Gambia to fulfil that vow. I'll take him home: home to his only child (that year he went home, he sired a child by mistake), home to his mother and to the rest of his family. Then he would be happy. His soul would rest in peace. Do you feel like I do? You will say I have always been the sentimental type. But then, it is not my fault that I feel the way I do. For once in my life, I want to do something selfless, something I stand to make no financial gains from. REALLY!

** **

It is quite late now, nearing midnight. Everywhere is as quiet as a graveyard. The sea has now calmed down, like a sated beast, like a vanquished enemy. I can even hear my wife and children's relaxed breathing in the bedroom. Outside, the sky is alive and crawling with brilliant silvery stars, and one of them has just unhinged, like an old door …and is falling, falling, scattering its silvery embers everywhere, falling fast towards my window… oh, what a beauty…a shooting star, Joe, a shooting star…I'm wishing now, wishing for good health for you and for myself and family, and long life for all of us…and prosperity too. Yes, prosperity!

** **

And talking about prosperity, are you now prosperous? Have you achieved your mind's desire of making bundles of money? That was your main aim of going to Europe. Remember? Or have your values, like mine, gone through a severe metamorphosis?

In spite of all the disappointments, from my failed European journey, to the 'white lies' of the prospects of the places in The Gambia called; 'German' and 'London', to the impotency of our great country to give meaning to the lives of her citizens; in spite of the pains of watching fellow Nigerians die and be buried like animals in far away countries while searching for greener pastures that their country could have otherwise comfortably provided; in spite of the humiliation we suffer for being what we are, 'Nigerians', I tell you, hope still lives in me.

Though if I say I'm thrilled at the way my life has turned out, I'll be lying. But I am not sad. I am not heartbroken. At least I have started a family. My wife Haddy and my three sweet kids are more blessings than I could ever wish for. Each of them is priceless.

But I'll leave it to you to decide if I've made progress or not, especially considering my age...our age. Sometimes I wonder how the forties caught up with us. So fast and so sudden, like a thief, a highway robber in a starless night.

My dear Joe, as a last word, I'll leave you with a quotation from *'Heirs to the Past',* a brilliant novel by a Moroccan novelist, Driss Chraibi, which I was privileged to read not long ago. Driss Chraibi wrote:
'Dig a well, and go down to look for water.
The light is not on the surface, but deep down.
Wherever you may be, even in the desert, you will always find water.
You have only to dig deep.'
I believe Driss, Joe, I believe him. My eyes are now open to understand what he was talking about. Does it make sense to you?

Remain blessed my dear friend. That we'll meet again is a forgone conclusion. The only question is where and when.

Write me again soon.

Your friend,

Tapha.

ll: 39 p.m.

I remember Syl and other stories

3

the 'Afinjang' Bishop

Unless you are a Gambian...or live in The Gambia, you wouldn't know what Afinjang is all about. So I will tell you. Afinjang is a Mandinka folkloric song made famous by the Gambian National Army Band during the last presidential election. The song tells of the nostalgia felt by a bride as she leaves her father's house for her matrimonial home, and the accompanying fanfare of dancing, flirting, teasing and merry making.

Afinjang is so heady, that no one is spared its allure and opiate power. Whenever it is vibrating over loudspeakers, the sick, the lame and the crippled become hungry for a dance...and actually dance!

Politicians love Afinjang, for it draws the electorate like honey draws flies. At rally centres, villages as well as market squares, before they commence their honed craft of making long-winded speeches, everyone must first dance to the magical Afinjang. If you were a visitor, you would be amazed, as, before your very eyes, a set of a dozen or more people would quickly commandeer, and form a circle around the enormous, corrugated trunks of nearby mango, silk-cotton, neem, orange and baobab trees. When the available trees are all occupied, people rally to the walls of nearby houses and shops. Or to the sides of vehicles or any standing object, say an electric or a telephone pole.

Spreading their legs, men and women, boys and girls, the old and the young would grab these upright objects and with eyes closed and mouths agape, rock their waists to the left...and to the right...and to the left...and to the right, front and back, front and back...in rhythm with the soul searing song. Giant bluebottles have been known to undertake reconnaissance trips inside these open mouths as their owners are held to ransom by the magnetic tunes of Afinjang, issuing forth from gigantic loudspeakers.

Afinjang is equally the darling of market women. Excited customers, with the song floating in their brains end up being cheated into the bargain. Touts love Afinjang; it engenders the ideal environment for pockets to be cleanly picked.

Even the clergy! They love Afinjang too!

In the middle of his favourite tripartite-themed sermon of 'Brood of vipers', 'Pharisees and Sadducees', and 'Whitewashed graves...sparkling on the outside, but stinking on the inside', my Lord Bishop would suddenly freeze, and then go limp, and for several long seconds, would rock his heavy rump (not unlike a woman's) first to the east, and then to the west and at last, with a frenzy, front and back, front and back, as a campaign vehicle zooms past, with Afinjang blaring from its loudspeakers. Rolling his bulgy eyeballs at his awe-stricken congregation, he would then mop his sweaty creased brow with one long, slim finger, flicking the brown sweat here and there, and, like the Biblical John the Baptist in the wilderness, he would go prancing to and fro on the altar and crying eloquently in his native Krio in a crazed, booming voice, "Yes!...Yes! Mi fambo. We God pikin dem need such tonics lek Afinjang na we lives."

The congregation, suddenly released from their trance would then go agog, prompting themselves with shouts of, "HALLELUUUUU..."

And the old cathedral, on its brick foundations, would rumble with an ear bursting, "HALLELUJAAAAHHH!"

Such is the fervour...such is the emotive power of Afinjang!

Now, maybe I should tell you more about my Lord Bishop, the Rt. Rev. Dr. Barr. Estrewaje. You should see him performing on stage: an overflowing robe, sometimes white, other times purple, complete with a Jewish skullcap, barely concealing his shimmering bald patch. Gold-rimmed spectacles, precariously perched on his broad, squashed nose, like a flesh-eating Palaeolithic bird about to swoop on an unsuspecting prey. Hanging on his neck is a gold crucifix, large enough to crucify an adult on; gold rings, adorned with multi-coloured stones grace all three last fingers of the left hand, and of course, the faithful solid silver Swiss chronometer! A peacock would surely asphyxiate with envy and jealousy, seeing Bishop Estrewaje, rainbow-like, as he trots, vibrates and spits 'holy' fire on his 'more-often-than-not', bemused congregation, especially when the warm early morning sun rays stealing through cracks on the ancient coloured glass windows of the old cathedral bath him in glorious colours, which is most of the time.

A born charlatan and title lover, Bishop Estrewaje!

Okay, he may be a gifted charlatan and title lover, and may have since cut his teeth as a dramatist and public speaker, but my Lord Bishop is a no-nonsense Bishop. True, you must give him that! You dare not make silly jokes with him. If you do, then you deserve what comes your way. If you are, say a foreign priest serving under his jurisdiction, and you mess around with his Holiness, you are given less than 24 hours to haul your priestly arse out of the country. You see, apart from priding himself as the Bishop that he rightly is, my Lord Bishop also likes to think of himself as the interior minister.

"Look," he would often bark at an offending priest, "I am the Bishop of Serrekunda, the largest Diocese in The Gambia. Do you realize that? There are only two people I care about in this country...the Chief Imam and His Excellency, the President..."

I cannot understand why my Lord Bishop would care for the Chief Imam, after all, are they not at loggerheads with respect to what Jesus really 'is' and the 'legitimacy' of Mohammed, whom my Lord Bishop has often described as an 'illegitimate' child, sired under sin? Well, that is not my bother, though I dare say I know why my Lord Bishop will care for His Excellency.

Once, His Excellency had given my Lord Bishop a very important national assignment. The sort that IBB[*] of Nigeria would give to somebody he wanted to discredit. Remember? IBB did it to Comrade Tai Solarin[+]...that archetype of the Indian leader, Mohandas Karamchand, aka Mahatma Gandhi. Comrade Tai Solarin later died after IBB had finished messing him up. Some people said he committed suicide to ram home his disgust for IBB!

Anyway, my Lord Bishop had wanted to keep a clean slate, but had underestimated His Excellency, a student of IBB.

"You want to spoil my hard earned revolution?" His Excellency had barked. "Do what I tell you, because I put you there."

"No. I am the Lord Bishop of Serrekunda. I must be seen to be fair," my Lord Bishop had barked in return.

"Then I sack you with immediate effect!" His Excellency announced on state radio and television.

"No you can't sack me. This is democracy," my Lord Bishop cried. "I must seek redress in our impeccable legal system," he told a sympathetic congregation one hot Sunday.

And, His Excellency, with 'ears' everywhere heard!

"You can seek redress in heaven for all I care," His Excellency fired back, this time in a state owned newspaper. "When I appointed you as the Chairman of the National Electoral Commission, you did not seek anything. Now I ask you to go, and you are seeking redress. Maybe you want six feet!"

---

[*] Former Nigerian military dictator, General Ibrahim Badamasi Babangida
[+] A well-known Nigerian nationalist and educationist, now late.

As soon as 'six feet' was mentioned, my Lord Bishop cowered. Not that he is a coward mind you, but then, who likes to be threatened with 'six feet below sea level'? Not even my Lord with all his undisguised love for heaven where honey and milk flows non-stop, and there is neither hunger nor thirst, pain nor sorrow, slavery nor injustice. My good Lord Bishop has every reason to reckon with His Excellency who can face America and Russia and Britain all rolled into one (...with his one and only refurbished jet fighter, a gift...or rather a bribe from some Asian country, seeking autonomy from the mighty 'Dragon').

When my Lord Bishop was not seeing himself as an interior minister or as a former NEC heavyweight, he was thinking of himself as a businessman.

"Actually," he would announce in church, pounding his chest like an angry gorilla, "I am more of a businessman than a clergy."

And this is absolutely true!

You want to cheat my Lord Bishop of a dime? Think again. Once, one of his priests had submitted a claim of a few dalasi for some church work he had carried out with his personal money. As if that was not enough, the 'thieving' priest, asked for a car to be assigned to him, and for a telephone to be installed in his house. And he was a foreign priest. A refugee to be specific.

What cheek!

You should have seen my Lord Bishop as he thundered like a tornado and tore like a tsunami:

"In Liberia where you come from, does your parish own even a spoke, not to talk of a bicycle? Now you want a car, a telephone, a computer, a gas cooker, a fax machine, a mobile phone, satellite dish, cable TV...You are taking advantage of my magnanimity, eh? Now pack and go back to your Liberia. You have 24 hours to vamoose."

Poor priest! In less than six hours, he was a double refugee, having been kicked out of the vicarage.

Hmm...

During the process of hoodwinking this poor priest into abandoning his native Diocese in Liberia, my Lord Bishop had promised everything under the sun; from a fully furnished apartment to refunds for any church work done with personal money and refunds of travel expenses. But of course, he had somehow forgotten these pledges.

My Lord? Whoever you may be, don't joke with him where money is concerned. What of one time when some mission partners had wanted to audit him? As it were, several thousands of US dollars donated for mission work had quickly developed limbs and strolled daintily out of the church's coffers.

"To question my impeccable integrity, what sacrilege? A whole Bishop like myself who answers to only two people in this universe? Now withdraw your nosey missionaries. You think this is colonial days? Don't you realise you should be paying reparations for enslaving my people and carting away our natural resources years ago when you brought your 'nonsensical' religion this way?"

Just like that. The Home Office in Ireland withdrew the poke-nosing missionaries and talks of the missing ten thousand USD died a natural death.

My Lord Bishop...expert craftsman. There is no auditing him. If you dare, try.

My Lord Bishop is an enigma. The youngest man to be ordained Bishop on planet earth...believe it or not. And an acclaimed sportsman too. A former member of the national table-tennis team, cricket team, lawn tennis team, handball team, basketball team, football team, you just name the team and he was there. He was even a member of the choir before he became bishop at his tender age, having 'somehow' muscled out his one and only opponent by threatening to tell the whole world 'something', if the opponent did not kindly 'step aside'.

Some say that he is not matured enough to hold such a sensitive post. They argue that since he assumed the position of bishop, three quarters of the congregation has disappeared, some becoming 'born again', others shifting to Catholicism, and yet others cross-carpeting, preferring to become Methodists and Baptists and even Muslims!

Not that my Lord Bishop cares.

As long as there were two or three 'suzies' tucked nicely away in a fancy hotel somewhere, preferably out of town to service him, and access to Guinness was not denied him, every other person could go to hell and roast there.

The last time there was a Father's Day celebration in the church, the hall was filled to capacity, bringing back sweet memories of good old days when parishioners had not deserted and became apostates. Guinness was flowing. The organizers had hired a DJ, and sweet music was flowing too. You should have seen my Lord Bishop in full glory, with a flowing regalia of purple frock coat. He cradled two chilled and sweating bottles of Guinness in both hands, prancing from one table to another and urging the young men, "Rise up brothers, rise. Dance. We must have a foretaste of our heavenly bounty here on earth."

And when one of James Brown's soul searing songs wafted out of the speakers, my Lord Bishop strode to a very beautiful woman, a parishioner's wife, and 'excused' her for a dance, whereupon he rested his large head on the unsuspecting woman's prominent cleavage, to her and her husband's chagrin and to the consternation of the parishioners who whispered their bewilderment of 'See the Bishop, see the Bishop,' in hushed tones.

But the evening was just beginning.

And the DJ had not forgotten to bring along a cassette of Afinjang.

Half way through the Father's Day, when parishioners who believed in the 'drink-but-don't-get-drunk' philosophy were well and truly soaked (not drunk, mind you), Afinjang suddenly rent the already charged atmosphere. And the crowd, including my Lord Bishop were thrown into a frenzy as they roared their approval. Quickly, everyone sought an upright object. Determined not to be outdone, my Lord Bishop, with his bottle spilling its black content raced to the nearest plum tree; he of course needed to have a vantage position.

And as the opiate tunes of Afinjang, together with alcohol seeped into his marrow and overtook his sensibilities, my Lord Bishop, grabbing his plum tree in one hand and his bottle in another rocked to the fierce rhythm.

Oh, what a sight!

What a spectacle!

Several minutes passed as Afinjang held sway.

The churchwarden, a teetotaller, and the Bishop's bodyguard so to speak, soon noticed the tears streaming down the Bishop's face in his ecstasy. He went over and gently pried the Bishop away, disarming him of his black bottle, as one would remove a candy from a sleeping child.

The warden then led the Bishop to his black jeep.

"Brood of vipers...Lepers...white washed tombs," astonished parishioners heard him whispering incoherently as he was being led away.

If only they knew why my Lord Bishop was weeping. If only they knew that the night before he had received a rather disturbing telephone call from his doctor. As his driver sped away, with him slumped in his owner's corner, the nightmare returned, and he cringed, blocking his ears with both hands. This however could not keep away his doctor's sombre voice, "Yes, I am sure your Lordship. The HIV test results came out positive again."

4

after the tea party

When the people of Banjul went to the news-stands that Saturday morning, they were told, 'there may be no papers today.' The people were angry. They wanted to know why might there be no papers today? Why can't they have ordinary papers to read? They insisted, 'we must have papers to read. How else can we know what is happening in our country if we have no papers to read. We must have papers to read.'

They gathered at the beginning of Independence Drive. They gathered at the centre of Picton Street. They gathered at the end of Marina Parade. They gathered at every street corner where papers were sold, waiting for the papers, or news of the papers. Sometimes, the papers came out late. But, it had never been this late. The time was well after nine. They waited, ready to scramble for the papers when they did arrive. Reading the papers was the only thing that kept them occupied over the weekends. The radios did not broadcast; their licences having been seized. The only radio that broadcast was the government radio. The people would rather listen to funeral songs than listen to the government radio. Watching TV was painful too. All that was shown in it was the President and his wife going to and coming from abroad on vacation. Or, commissioning one 'white elephant' project after another. Or, from their state-of-the-art farm harvesting watermelon and pumpkins, farmed with machinery that the ordinary farmer was yet to set his eyes.

In readiness for the scrambling which they hoped to do, the old men pulled up their sleeves as they eyed the young men who flexed their muscles. At exactly ten o'clock, they were told, 'The papers won't be coming at all.'

'The paper is our only eye,' the people cried in one voice. 'What is wrong?'

'Everything,' the newsvendor, just arriving from the press said, 'everything is wrong.'

'Pray, tell us something,' the people pleaded. 'You are frightening us with your talk.'

'Everything is wrong,' the vendor repeated, shaking his head.

'Should we pack our belongings and families and leave town then?'

'Last night, they killed DH,' the vendor announced. 'That is why the papers will not be coming out today. Or, even tomorrow.'

The people were confused. They searched each other's faces. They found no answers there.

'Pray, tell us,' they cried, 'who is this DH? Who killed him? What was his crime?'

'It was last night that they shot him dead in Serrekunda as he drove home after the tea party.'

That was all the answer the newsvendor could offer. The people were more confused now. They wanted to know what tea party. But the newsvendor had disappeared. He slinked into one dark alley, out of sight, his empty bag slung over his shoulder. The people began to talk in hushed voices. They didn't understand at all. Was there an attempted coup last night? But who was this DH? Why would killing him prevent the newspapers from coming out? Instead, the papers ought to appear to tell people about the killing and why he was killed and who killed him. The papers were not doing their job properly, the people concluded. They began to disperse into Grant Street and Allen Street and Macdonald Street and all the other streets from which they had come. Perhaps the government-controlled radio would give details about this DH and why he was killed. They would go to their radios to learn what there was to learn. But they did not have any hope of learning the truth. Not from the government radio. Or, TV.

Later that day, around noon, the streets began filling with men wearing battle fatigues. Trucks painted in camouflage dropped them at fifty meters intervals around Banjul. They looked fierce, some bearing AK 47 guns, others SMGs. They did not smile. Their eyes were bloodshot. Their heads were protected with heavy helmets. Their black boots shone. Afraid, the people asked themselves, 'Is our country expecting a foreign invasion?' Soon, the streets emptied. Parents rushed to the various playgrounds to withdraw their children. The traders of Albert market locked up their stalls and rushed home. Public transport operators parked their buses and taxis at home. In Serrekunda, the commercial heart of the country, the pandemonium in Banjul was re-enacting itself.

Rumours filled the air: Coup! A coup was attempted last night. This DH was the ringleader. The government is searching for two women, thought to be his co-plotters. Transistor radios crackled everywhere. People tuned to the BBC and RFI hoping to hear something. Nobody heard anything.

The government had reasons posting military and anti-riot police everywhere around the city. Intelligence reports reaching them had said, 'The people are planning a huge demonstration.' The government knew that they must not let the demonstration hold. It would create a conducive atmosphere for looting and mayhem. They must protect the citizenry. 'Shoot any demonstrator at sight,' the men bearing guns had been ordered. 'You are indemnified.'

****

A huge hush had since permeated the six newspaper houses scattered around Banjul and Serrekunda. Reporters preferred to hang outside their newspaper houses. Most unclipped their press cards from around their necks and breast pockets, finding better places for them inside bags and purses and drawers and brassieres. They avoided the stern gaze of the military who crawled everywhere like vermin. Inside *Narr* (Mauritanian) shops and Ghanaian bars they hung out, talking in low tones, heads touching, eyes shifting, not trusting anyone, even members of their fourth estate.

'What exactly happened?'

'I don't know the full details.'

'But what did you hear?'

'That a strange saloon car with tinted glasses and without plate numbers overtook them and blocked their way somewhere in Kanifing. Then, two men wearing hoods bounced out and approached their car. The two men shot DH through the head. He died instantly.'

'I heard that there were two of his junior workers with him.'

'The ladies managed to escape.'

'Where are they now?'

'Hiding in one of the western embassies.'

'Which one?'

'Nobody is saying.'

'I heard the secret police is searching frantically for them. What for?'

'To eliminate them.'

'What do you mean?'

'They are too dangerous to be left unattended.'

'You don't mean the government-'

'They had the motives. He wrote too much against them. He challenged their every decision. He was against the Media Commission Bill. He was against the Newspaper Amendment Act. He criticised the way they handled the last trading season, robbing the farmers of their produce, paying them peanuts for their peanut. He said the bye-election in Bakau was rigged in favour of the ruling party. They had every reason to silence him, especially as another general election is around the corner.'

'But there is no proof that the government was responsible.'

'Are you looking for a proof?'

'He may have been involved in a shady deal.'

'That is what the government is saying. That a business associate he cheated may have done him in. Already they are holding a Nigerian.'

'You don't say!'

'Who does that mad dictator and his henchmen think they are fooling?'

****

By 7 p. m. that evening, the slain body of the veteran journalist, DH, was lying at the morgue in the Teaching Hospital in the centre of Banjul. It was riddled with bullet holes. Members of union of journalists counted eighteen such bullet holes. His nose and eyes and mouth were occluded with blood. Only one half of his head remained, the other having been blown away. No one had touched the body since it was brought in and deposited on the floor last night. They were waiting for the chief pathologist to come back from the province where he had gone for official matters. Only the chief pathologist could say the cause of death. The government was determined: for security reasons, only the chief pathologist will be the first to examine the body and give a verdict about the cause of death. But no one was in doubt about the cause of death.

'But, at least, give the man some respect,' the union leader pleaded. 'Preserve the body in the fridge.'

'Some vital evidence may be lost which may jeopardise the investigation we hope to mount for his killer, or killers,' the chief of secret police said.

'The body is already decomposing. His flesh is torn in several places.'

'We will wait for the chief pathologist to return,' the chief of secret police insisted.

That night, members of the Union of Journalists gathered at the union headquarters in Kairaba Avenue. They decided to assemble the next day at eight for a march to statehouse, Banjul. Government must be pressured into hunting for the killer or killers of their fearless brethren. They assigned responsibilities quickly: a communiqué was quickly drafted. To be typed and sent to the various diplomatic missions that same night. Vests bearing a smiling picture of the late DH to be printed overnight and distributed to journalists the next morning, the route of the planned match to be determined the next day. Before they could conclude their plans proper, the meeting was broken up by secret police.

'If you want to hold a meeting,' the officer in charge of the operation said, 'you must first get clearance from headquarters.'

Thanks to cell phone and the accompanying text message facility, news of the march was well publicised. It was a large, but peaceful gathering the next day: journalists and non-journalists alike, jobless youths, market women, taxi and bus drivers. The crowd brandished placards, many of which read:

WHO KILLED DH?
BRING THE COWARDS TO BOOK
A DEAD PRESS, A DEAD COUNTRY
TIME SHALL UNMASK THE TRUTH

The murder of the popular journalist had attracted so much attention. Overnight, foreign press had sneaked into the country, thanks to the porous borders. The government decided that for the sake of democracy, the journalists' march should be allowed to hold. Not that they could have done much to prevent it. The cameras were already rolling, feeding TV stations all over the world.

At statehouse in Banjul, the Minister of the Interior and Inspector General of Police were at hand to receive the grieving journalists. Both men were dressed for the occasion: the Minister in an impeccable, flowing white Caftan, his companion in starched black shirt, black trousers, police cap, glittering medals, staff and all. Both men were nearly crying, dabbing at their eyes every now and then with handkerchiefs as they took turns to make their eloquent speeches: the state regrets the senseless killing of such a high profile journalist as DH, both men said. He was a fine gentleman; a true son of the soil; a fearless defender of human rights; a pure democrat. He fought for equality, for fairness, for good governance. Government had already put machinery in motion to apprehend the culprits, the cowards who perpetrated such a barbaric act. When caught, they would face the full weight of the law. Citizens should go back to their businesses. Their security was guaranteed. No cause for alarm. Everyone was touched.

Both men fielded questions from the press:

"'How soon can the people expect result?'"

"'As soon as possible.'"

"'Last time a vocal, high profile Supreme Court judge was shot through the heart at close quarters in Manjaikunda, the government promised to track the killers as soon as possible. Ten months have flown by, still the public has been told nothing."

"'That is because investigations are still on going and to be more specific, things have not gone smoothly because the public has failed to cooperate and assist the police. How can the police do their work properly if the citizenry fold their hands?"

"'People are pointing accusing fingers at the government for the murder of the veteran journalist, DH-"

"'Such accusations are baseless. What use is a dead lion to anyone? The government stands to gain more with a living DH than with a dead DH. DH was a stern opposition of the government. The government welcomes opposition from all fronts. That is what democracy is all about, isn't it?"

The protesters went home more confused. That night, unidentified men torched the house of the RFI stringer in Brufut, thirty kilometres from Banjul. While the meeting was going on at statehouse, the stringer was prowling town, poking his dirty nose where it did not belong; letting every ignorant Tom, Dick and Harry talk into his useless microphone. Who did he think he was, brandishing his tape recorder here and there and everywhere? If he wanted to learn the facts, did he not know the way to statehouse? His Excellency, the President would have granted him audience. Who was in the best position to know how the slain journalist was killed if not the Chief Commander, His Excellency, the President who was constantly briefed about state matters? The RFI stringer was lucky to escape through a side window. He fled the country that same night through the southern border. Unbeknown to him, at precisely that moment he was criss-crossing through the forest disguised as a hunter, the editors of the Daily Chronicle and the Herald were making their ways out of the country through the eastern and northern borders respectively, one disguised as a farmer, the other a trader. The Daily Chronicle and the Herald, together with DH's paper, 'Salt of the Nation' were the most fervent antagonists of the ruling party.

****

DH was a big man; so full of life. He was a man who did not like to be complimented. But for once he laughed, acknowledging the compliment being showered on him. It was a laugh that emanated from the bottom of his stomach: full, throaty, resounding. It carried all over the newsroom, venue of the tea party. The young men and women present halted in mid action and mid sentences, throwing the room into silence. Only the throaty laugh of the big man remained. The big man was their boss. They stole a glance at him; and smiled encouragingly. They loved him. They respected him. He was their mentor, their father. They saw his potbelly struggling against an undersized packet shirt heave up and down as he laughed; his red silk tie threatening to choke him. A thin film of tear coated his bloodshot eyes, hidden behind thick medicated glasses. They resumed their hushed discussion, none daring to speak too loud. They knew it would be rude; the ambassador of the United States was their guest.

'I mean it,' the ambassador said again to the big man. 'You have courage. Great courage.'

The big man removed his glasses. He dabbed his eyes several times with a piece of white cloth from his breast pockets. Then he polished the glasses with the white cloth. He polished for a long time. The ambassador watched and waited. The big man threw his head back and laughed again; this time for only a brief moment.

'You have to be courageous,' the big man said.

'But-'

'No buts,' the big man said, looking at the ambassador squarely in the face. The big man was all seriousness now. 'You have to have courage to do the kind of work we do. We are fighting against the system.'

'The system is bad.'

'That would be putting it mildly. The system is stinking. It is fouling everywhere and everybody: the innocent, the hard working, the unborn, humanity. The system is enslaving us. We must fight it.'

'But your methods-'

'That is the only way I know. How else can I. . .how else can we hope to boot out dictatorship if not by that means. They have the guns and gun batteries. We have the pen and paper.'

'Some say you are maligning him. Because he is from a minority tribe.'

'You mean His Excellency, the President?'

'Yes.'

The big man was silent. The ambassador waited. Time crawled. The big man inched forward in his seat, took one of the ambassador's hands, rubbed it warmly for awhile. Releasing it, the big said in a hushed tone:

'What do you say, Mr. Ambassador? What do you say?'

It was the big man's strategy to court the sympathy of all western diplomats. He was on first name terms with the ambassadors of Britain, France, Russia, Germany. He was on first name terms with the ambassador of the Vatican. He had been on first name terms with the just gone ambassador of the United States, Ambassador Schultz. Now, he hoped to be on first name terms with Dr. Hill Freeman who only just arrived as a replacement. The tea party, held at DH's 'Salt of the Nation' offices in Kairaba Avenue was his idea to win Dr. Freeman over.

53

The ambassador, an Emeritus Professor of International Relations knew he had been cornered. He sipped his tea; his brow furrowed. The big man watched and waited. He smiled encouragingly. He said to the ambassador:

'Dr. Freeman, be free. This is an informal gathering, in your honour. I can never quote you.'

'No, no, no,' the ambassador protested. 'I wasn't thinking of being quoted. You are a gentleman-'

'Oh yes I am a gentleman.'

Both men laughed, the mounting tension diffusing.

'More tea?'

'Oh no, thank you,' the ambassador said, relieved; he had been saved from giving his personal opinion about the ebullient editor. He wasn't sure how Washington would have reacted.

Later the ambassador gave an eloquent speech. He played it safe, extolling democracy and pointing out its fruits. In no uncertain terms, he condemned the enemies of democracy; he condemned those who with impunity inflicted pain and suffering on the poor and unsuspecting masses. The big man, as usual was fearless. He condemned his country's government for its disrespect of democracy; italicised and underlined its poor human rights records, its looting of the public treasury; asked the ambassador of the United States to encourage his country to institute sanctions against the ruling class.

The tea party dispersed by 10 p.m. By half past eleven, the big man was dead, his robust body riddled with bullets from unlicensed, automatic sub-machine guns; his two young female companions scampering blindly through the thick undergrowth, not sure if their pretty skulls had been hit or not. Left to mourn him were his young wife, seven months pregnant and his cataract-troubled aged mother. Had he lived another two days, DH would have celebrated his forty-eight birthday.

*****

The Union of Journalists agreed to suspend publication and transmission for one week. To honour their fallen hero, their father and mentor, they said. The government, through DOSI, the Department of State for Information, sent out a strongly worded memo. The memo advised all journalists working in its establishment not to partake in any such boycott of rewarding work. Any journalist disregarding the injunction would be summarily dismissed. Equally, the memo reminded the other privately owned media houses of the duty they owed the public to publish news worth reading and not likely to incite public disobedience. One day spent in peaceful demonstration was enough homage to their fallen member. Staying away from work for one week would be tantamount to relinquishing their licenses to operate as media houses.

At the Union headquarters in Kairaba Avenue, the journalists discussed their dilemma. DH was dead and gone, resting in the bosom of the Lord, they said. They had families to cater for. What was the use of losing their sources of livelihood if it would not bring the good DH back from the river beyond? They must resume publications to avoid losing their bread. Besides, DH would never have approved of the idea of newspapers being off the stands for so long on his account. He was that selfless.

In a simple ceremony, DH was buried at the Christian cemetery in the capital, Banjul. The event was well attended. Dressed in a black suit and trouser and a matching white tie, Dr. Freeman, the ambassador of the United States of America wore a long face all through the solemn ceremony. He had come to admire and love the slain newspaperman, even referring to him as, 'A close friend.'

DH's grave was a simple grave. The government forbade the placement of a befitting epitaph.

'It may incite unrest,' the government spokeswoman said.

'How?' the Union of Journalists wanted to know.

The journalists insisted they must have a befitting epitaph, to immortalise their father. 'Well, if you want an epitaph for your overzealous hero, you can have it,' the spokeswoman capitulated. 'But first you will have to get clearance from the Inspector General's office.'

The Union of Journalists buried their dead without an epitaph. And determinedly, with heads held high, shoulders raised, chests thrust out, blood hammering in veins, they trudged back to their newspaper houses and to their writing desks. They told themselves:

'More than anything else, we must write. We must publish.'

And write and publish they did. For one long week, each newspaper house came out with forty pages of newsprint, printing at least fifty thousand copies. Each media house chose one of six slogans, splashing it, together with a smiling photograph of their slain hero across the entire forty pages. The slogans, done against black backgrounds read:

O DEATH, WHERE IS THY STING; O GRAVE, WHERE IS THY
 VICTORY?
YOU CAN'T FOOL ALL THE PEOPLE ALL THE TIME
TIME SHALL UNMASK THE TRUTH

A DEAD PRESS, A DEAD COUNTRY
BRING THE COWARDS TO BOOK
WHO KILLED DH?

For seven long days, the people trooped out in their multitudes to buy; addicts of newspaper and non-addicts alike. Some for the purpose of beholding the smiling face of the dead journalist. Others to keep as souvenirs to show their children, yet unborn.

friends since armitage days

Most times, I like slinking away. The endless banter of my kids and infighting between their mothers is hell and can drive a man crazy.

For the past two weeks, I have been holed up in Gondola Camp. This time however, neither because of my kids nor my wives. I am in a UN workshop. Alone at the cafeteria, I dig into the fried lump of barracuda on my plate, wishing the workshop would last forever. Moments later as I wash down my barracuda with chilled beer, a shadow from behind falls across my plate. Before I can look back, a hand clasps my left shoulder. I almost choke. Who the hell can be playing this expensive joke with me?

"Dear me, dear me," I burst out on taking in the clean-shaven face with sparkling white, not too even teeth peeping out of robust lips. "How nice to see you. I missed you, man."

"I missed you too," James says, the sound emanating from somewhere deep in his belly.

Old pals that we are, we embrace and pat each other's back like we always do whenever we meet. Hearing us talk of missing each other, one gets the impression that we have not seen one another for aeons. But it is exactly a fortnight ago that we drank beer until midnight at the Monument. James ended up drinking six instead of his usual three bottles. I drove him home in his car, and then came back in a taxi for my jalopy, a Renault 3. The following morning, I took off for Gondola.

"What brings you here, business?" I say, pulling a chair for him. "Join me please, let's share my fried fish."

Sitting down opposite me, James shakes his head slowly. No thanks, he says. He has had something to eat. His eyes are puffy and bloodshot. I think, Lack of sleep. His Afro hair, usually well combed, is ruffled. A few black stains present themselves on his silk tie, which hangs askew. Coffee. James is a coffee addict. He drinks it neat all day. He has become a Frenchman by association and speaks the language fluently.

"Beer then?" I say.

"Coffee."

Wiping my mouth and moustache with serviette, I push remnants of my lunch aside and beckon to a waitress. She rushes forward as if given a violent push from behind. She is young, seventeen, maybe eighteen. Supple. She is probably new on the job.

"A cup of coffee for this gentleman please," I say. "No sugar."

"Sir, we have run out of coffee."

"Let's drink beer then, James. What do you say?"

James says nothing.

"Eh, James? What do you say?"

Still no reply.

His eyes are focused on something in the distance. I follow his gaze. I make out a dozen or so pelicans scattered on the brown waters of the slow flowing river, fishing. Steam rises from the water, gives the surface a fizzy appearance. I shift my eyes to the riverbanks. It is low tide. Black mud is spread as far as the eye can see; hundreds of jagged rocks and stones litter everywhere. The shrieks of two kingfishers colliding in mid air reach our ears. We raise our heads. Our eyes seek and locate them as they fly their separate ways, the black of their feathers shimmering against the sunlight, burning in the cloudless sky. One of the kingfishers rises far into the sky, turns head down, folds his wings neatly and swoops down with lightening speed, crashing into the liquid brownness, spraying water. I start violently. In a jiffy, he is out of the water, a struggling crayfish between his beaks.

I exhale slowly.

James isn't admiring the scenery. The fancy comes to me that he is ill.

"Get us six bottles of beer," I say to the waitress who is struggling not to look James's way. I point to a grass hut by the edge of the river where it is supposed to be cooler. "Bring the beers over there."

"Sir, ice cubes?" the waitress says.

"Lots," I say.

I nudge James lightly on the ribs. He shows me his teeth: an attempt at smiling. My heart goes out to him.

The beers arrive. I watch James. He opens one, empties the entire 280ml into his tumbler, and tosses the bottle into the river. The bottle bobs about for a few seconds, swallows water, and begins to sink. Bubbles from it rise to the surface. James swirls the contents of his tumbler a bit, isn't happy with the result; starts to use one long finger to mix the beer and ice cubes, changes his mind; licks the finger; takes one long swallow, stares into the distance.

I take a sip straight from my bottle, smack my lips not too loudly, and feel my moustache. It isn't wet. I rub it down; sort of flatten the hair to keep them slick. Under normal circumstances, James isn't to be rushed. The circumstance as I see now is abnormal. His business rarely brings him outside the diplomatic circle in the city. I wait. I have the patience of a professional salesman. The riverbank smells. I try placing the odour. I can only arrive at the smell of sex. I see James wrinkle his nose. I do the same. That night at the Monument, I hadn't ascribed James's drunkenness to anything unusual. As I think about it now, I begin to wonder, Have I been paying enough attention to my childhood friend?

Time passes.

"How would you define faithfulness?" James says, startling me. His voice is scarcely audible. I feel like a deadly wasp has stung me. I need to clear my head. I stall for time by picking my nose. James lets me think.

"You mean being faithful?" I say after a while.

"Yes, being faithful."

"To what?"

"To one's partner."

"Is Carol...," I begin, then change my mind. Instead I say, "Why do you ask?"

"Don't answer my question with question."

"I've to know why before I can give a responsible answer," I say. "I've to know the particulars."

James broods. I know he is thinking about my use of the word, 'particulars', as if I am a traffic policeman: driver, let me see your particulars. My brain formulates and discards one definition of 'faithfulness' after another. It must have dispensed with more than a hundred such definitions.

"Faithfulness...being faithful, you say, it's a bit more complex...more complicated than you can imagine," I say.

"That is not a definition," James says. "And you know it," he ends, his nostrils flaring.

"Look, I can hardly give you a reasonable answer unless I know why you are asking," I say.

"I'm not a happy man," he says to me.

Under normal circumstances, I would have said to him, 'James dear, you are a big fool.' But I say:

"You make me laugh."

"You think because I've a good paying job-"

"And wonderful children-"

"And wonderful children …and know people in high places, I should be happy?"

"You are not even forty-five yet, see what you have already achieved in life," I say, my voice suddenly rising. "God has spread mayonnaise on both sides of your bread and you say you are not happy. What do you want people like me to say, or are you mocking me? James, did you travel all the way to this secluded resort to mock me?"

I spit into the river, watch the white foam float away; take a generous swig from my beer; check my anger. I rub down my moustache, make it slick. James leaves his beer alone, wrings his fingers, looks confused.

"All that you have so quickly enumerated does not make one truly happy?" he says.

"Besides, you have such a pretty wife, Carol. Shapely, tall, unbleached like most women out there, my wives included."

"Yes. Carol is very pretty. Ever since I set eyes on her in Armitage, I've not stopped marvelling at her beauty."

"You don't know how lucky you are, James. Sometimes, I wish you and I could swap places, for a few days, even hours."

"You don't know what you are talking about."

"But I do."

"Don't ever wish you were in my fucking shoes."

James voice is loaded with regret. I am instantly alarmed.

"Why?" I say, my voice dropping to a whisper.

"I'm suffering."

I am convinced now that James is sick. I take a closer look at him. His hairline seems to have receded several inches. His cheeks look hollow. Are my eyes playing tricks on me?

"James, are you ill or something?" I say.

"I'm perfectly healthy."

"Carol isn't sick or something, is she?"

"Depends on what you mean."

"But I saw her only last two weeks …with Susan."

Time passes as James digests this piece of information.

"Tell me," he says suddenly, "how well do you know Susan?"

"You ask me that question?" I say. "She is your wife's best friend, isn't she? They have been best friends since Armitage days."

"Susan isn't married."

This is an undisguised accusation

"Ever wondered why?" he says further.

"James, that is hardly my business," I say. "Besides, not every woman wants to be shackled to one man for life, you know."

"That is hardly the point."

"What then is the point?"

"Ever seen her with a man before, I mean going out for a date or being chatted up, fondled for example?"

I uncork another beer for myself, take a generous swallow.

"One for me, please," James says.

I open another for him. He takes a long swig. Out in the water, some pelicans take off from further afield, land nearby; others take off from nearby, fly several meters, land exactly where the first set had taken off from.

"Not exactly," I say after a while.

"Not exactly what?"

"I have never really seen Susan being fondled, for example."

"That is exactly the point, damn it."

"What exactly are you getting at?"

"When I think of it now as I've been doing every passing minute lately, ever since Armitage days, I never saw Susan with guys, not during our out nights, or times when we visited other schools for games or quiz contests. Carol was the only person you ever saw her with. Remember we wondered why?"

I say nothing. James continues, serious as a church.

"They ate together, slept together, had their baths together, studied together. At night when they stepped in dark areas, they quickly reached for each other, held hands. When we asked them-"

"But you were happy with the arrangement then... seeing that being together always, other boys couldn't play pranks with your Carol."

"But, after Armitage, they still remained inseparable."

"Isn't that what being good friendship is all about, being there for each other always?"

"Something happened in Armitage that I never told you. I never thought it meant anything until recently."

"Probably worrying yourself silly for nothing."

For several seconds, James looks at me from the corner of his eyes, as if to say, "Don't tell me you are so naïve."

I look away. He goes on:

"Once, I caught Carol and Susan having a heated argument. The only time I had seen them doing that. I had promised to meet Carol in our usual reading corner, near the old mango tree. Somehow, I had come earlier than I said I would. Approaching, I overheard voices. I was going to rush forward to stop any fight when I recognised the voices. I hid behind a disused oil drum and tried to listen. They began speaking in hushed tones.

Susan suddenly began to weep. Bitterly. I was shocked. As abruptly as she had begun, she stopped, wiped her tears with the back of her right hand. I heard Carol say: 'Nothing will come out of it, Sussy. Nothing, not even marriage can tear us apart. We will always remain what we are to each other.'

"They hugged each other, pecked themselves lightly on both cheeks."

I take a long swig from my bottle to hide my embarrassment. I watch a pelican fly past overhead. As if on cue, others flap their wings noisily, spraying water, rise to the sky and disappear. Another kingfisher, probably that first fellow falls into the water again. He emerges and flies away, screaming. I wonder if he has impaled himself on an unsuspecting rock. He didn't even catch his crayfish.

"Look, James," I say trying to sound brave but failing miserably, "there is nothing to what you witnessed. Girls feel that way when a guy comes out of the blues to mess up their friendship. Since we are being frank with each other, I might as well let you know that I too felt bad when you married Carol. It wasn't easy making new friends."

"Ours was different."

"I don't see how. Carol and Susan felt for each other what you and I felt."

"But you have since found your life, haven't you? For instance, you are married with two wives and children of your own. You have other friends and don't always need me around you always. But Susan continues to hang around my wife. Women normally drift apart when one gets married and the other does not. For Carol and Susan, the reverse is the case. Even now, Carol can't take a leak without Susan watching, as if they are joined at the hip or something. Believe it or not, on our wedding day, Susan cried."

"She had every right to. You stole her best friend."

"Her best friend, indeed."

"Look James, give the girls a break, will you. Is that why you are not happy, that your wife continues to be friendly with her old time chum who unfortunately isn't married?"

"To hell with you. You are beginning to sound as if I look down on Susan because she is not married."

"That is how any objective person would see it."

"You don't understand."

"I do. Unless there are some other things you have not told me."

"Let me ask you something, tell me, are you free with Binta and Sainabou?"

"My wives?"

"Yes, Your wives. Are you free with them?"

"Am I free with my wives? ...what do you mean, am I free with my wives? What kind of question is that?"

"What I mean is this...do they allow you to do everything ...anything ...I mean ...you know what I mean with them?"

"Of course, they do. They are my wives. Yes, I can do whatever I want with either of my wives."

"That is the point!"

"I don't get it."

"I can't go all the way with my Carol. I er... just er... enter and come, that is all. And even that is a rare phenomenon."

"What? No foreplay?"

"She doesn't allow it. No foreplay. Nothing like foreplay."

"How do you manage? Where is the fun then?"

"You are beginning to see what I mean when I say I'm not happy...all these seventeen years of marriage, I've been suffering."

"I feel for you if that is the case."

"Let me tell you what I witnessed some months back. Perhaps you will be able to advise me, because I'm about to run mad."

We both sip our beers slowly, each in deep thought. Cool wind begins to blow from across the river. The tide is rising. Tadpoles and crabs scramble to get a place on the parts of the rocks and stones not yet overtaken by the rising waters. That is why the pelicans flew away, I think. They know the tide is rising.

"About six months ago," James begins, "I rushed home from work, quite unlike me to go back home after leaving for work. It was 10 o'clock or thereabouts. Carol was supposed to be home alone. She had said she wasn't feeling too well to go to work. I wanted to give her a pleasant surprise then. I began to tiptoe towards our bedroom window. I was almost there when I heard the moaning."

Here, James stops. I wait, anxious for him to continue. When he continued brooding, I say:

"I am listening, James."

"I froze instantly on my tracks," he says. "I thought, in my house? On my matrimonial bed? I wanted to turn back and go far, far away, but I couldn't find the will power. Plucking courage, I peeped into the room. Scattered everywhere were articles of my wife's underclothes. And some stuff I never thought she could ever possess, or that I would ever find in my house. I then caught sight of a pair of man's jeans, a size 38."

"My God," I say unable to withstand the tension. I take a deep breath, forced air through my mouth.

"A closer peep into the room revealed my present nightmare. On the bed were the two bodies, entangled, oblivious to the world. Kissing. Caressing. Loving each other passionately. Then I saw a hand pass between Carol's thighs and a finger disappeared inside her. She allowed it without any retort, moaning at the top of her voice. I died. Such intimacy was a privilege I had longed for since I married Carol. As if that wasn't enough, I watched the other fellow nibble every crest of her body. Gradually, a head was buried between Carol's legs. Carol sang with ecstasy. All my life, I had never had the privilege of hearing my wife cry so. Sudden jealousy blinded me. Then I took a closer look at this light-skinned robust fellow with well-cropped hair violating my own wife in my own bedroom. When I saw who this fellow was, bile rose to my mouth and I fled, mad as a rabid dog.

"As soon as I was in the privacy of my car, I vomited all over the dashboard. Then I drove off like a man the devil was after. Like a man possessed by evil spirits. I didn't return to the office. How could I? And I had a diplomatic meeting to chair; I had just been made the Dean of the Diplomatic Corps. I kept driving. I drove to Old town. From Old town, I drove to Market Road, Traffic light. I crossed the ferry to Bodo. Coming back from Bodo, I drove to Ring Road. I took any road devoid of traffic. My cell phone kept ringing. My pager kept beeping. My head was full. I wanted to drink rat poison."

"Thank God you didn't."

"I wanted to drive my car into the river."

"She was cheating on you," I say as if the fact was not already obvious.

"That is what I wanted to know when I asked you to define 'faithfulness' for me."

"What?" I cry. "You caught your wife on your bed in your house with a fellow and-"

"And I've known that fellow all my life."

"Do I know this fellow?" I say, straightening up and staring James in the face. To steady my nerves, I take a long swig from my bottle. James sips his beer too, spilling half of the content. Then he says:

"Yes, you know this fellow." His voice shook.

"Who was he?" I say.

"This fellow wasn't a 'he'."

"What do you mean, 'fellow wasn't a he'?"

"It was Susan."

Silence takes possession of us. My thoughts roam: Susan? Dear God. James, I hope you are not bumming.

"I'm so sorry James," I say, ending the screaming silence.

James rubs a tear. My heart breaks. I bring out my handkerchief, place it where he can reach it. I gaze into the distance. I make out workshop participants trooping to the conference room. They can go this session without me, I think. We sit there a long time staring at the river, at our feet, at the sky, saying nothing; looking everywhere but at each other. The chill begins to set in.

"Let's go to my room," I say.

I lead the way. James follows. We stay up the whole night, not saying much to each other.

James leaves the next day. As I escort him to his car, people recognise him.

"I'll come next week for a Shengan visa," someone says jokingly.

"Diplomats," another says loud enough for everyone to hear. "Such easy lives."

I smile. James smiles too.

"I've borne the burden of this knowledge all alone since," James says as he starts his Lexus, the engine purring contentedly. "I needed to talk to someone. You will forgive me for...for crashing in on you like I did. I hope I have not ruined your 'Capacity Building' workshop."

I had found no single counsel to offer James. The thought killed me. That night and the following four nights, I toss and turn on my bed.

As soon as I get back, I go to see James in his office. Before him is a steaming jug of coffee. His porcelain cup is half empty. He is unusually chatty.

Did I care for some coffee?

No I didn't. Thank you.

He brewed it himself, couldn't wait for his secretary. Coffee was good for me. Didn't I say I was watching my potbelly? Caffeine would burn off the excess fat. He read it somewhere. Couldn't remember where exactly.

He suddenly stops talking, cocks his head as if to listen. I too cock my head to listen. The hum of the central AC carries through from outside. A clock ticks away by the far wall. In the outer office, James's secretary's UPS beeps. Her computer keys clatters away merrily.

"So what are you going to do now?" I say when we had both relaxed, content that no one is eavesdropping on us.

"I've not an inkling," he says.

"Women are deep."

"All these years."

We both fall silent. An eerie feeling envelope us.

"When I came back from visiting you at Gondola," he says, "I met up with Susan. She was just leaving my house. She had an overnight bag. The children confirmed that she spent the night there. I've been blind all these years. You know, she always came to keep Carol company when I was away on tour."

James sighs. My Adam's apple bobs up and down. We think our different thoughts.

"Will you put her away?" I say after a while.

"I'm a Roman Catholic."

"Surely, the priest would understand."

"Carol's folks would say I had found someone else. That I was giving a dog a bad name to justify its death."

"Ban Susan from your home," I say. "Break them up."

As soon as it leaves my mouth, I am sick at heart for making this suggestion. Break them up? Impudent old fool that I am, not to have held my silly tongue. Abysmal old windbag that I am. But I am angry. I feel betrayed too. Carol is a woman I hold up there.

In the distance, a car starts, revs its engine, and screeches away, the noise fading with it.

"Breaking them apart would hardly solve the problem," James says. "Neither would banning Susan from my house."

I nod.

"It's an integral part of their elements now," I say.

James bangs the table suddenly, startling me and upsetting his cup of coffee.

"Point is," he says through gritted teeth, "what the hell do I do with Carol? James please tell me?"

I sigh, swallow hard, and exhale deeply, my shoulders drooping. I had no counsel whatsoever to offer James. The shame gags me.

Two weeks later, James confronts Carol. It is in my presence.

"Can't trust myself to face her alone," he had said when I protested about being present during the confrontation.

"I'm sorry if I've disappointed you," Carol opens her defence. "I tried to warn you long ago, but you wouldn't listen. Sussy and I've something special. Besides, I've been a good wife to you. "

"By bringing a slut to make out on our matrimonial bed?" James says.

Tempers flare.

"Don't call her a slut," Carol says, the sound issuing from her lips like steam from a geyser.

"She is nothing but a slut. A fucking..."

A hush falls over us. James bows his head, cradles it in both hands. He is ashamed. I am embarrassed. I bow my head too.

Carol breaks the silence.

"Then I'm a slut, you mean?"

"Look, look, James, Carol, this wasn't why we arranged for this small get-together," I say for lack of something better.

"What do you know about this?" Carol shouts at me, her eyes blazing. "Keep out. Stay out of it."

My eyes smart. With determination, I ignore my armpits, which itch badly.

"You have ruined my life," James says, still holding his head.

"Your life! Your life!" Carol cries.

"Don't my life matter? I'm sorry if you see it that way, that I've ruined your life, but there is nothing I or anybody can do about it. Think of me, think, both of you. If I had my way, I could have happily stayed out of a heterosexual marriage. I'm not as strong willed as Sussy. Besides, her folks understand. Okay, maybe because she is a half-caste, what with her mother being a European. My parents would never have taken it. Accepting that I was different would have killed them. You don't know how I've suffered all these years. Hiding. Fretting. Looking out of the window, behind my back, expecting to find you, the kids, relatives, people, staring wide-eyed as Sussy and I touched. Or, kissed. Since we became husband and wife, I've lived through hell. Don't you see? You only think about yourselves. Men! Where is the love you have for me, James? This is the time to prove it. Prove it now, that you really love me!"

Carol is shaking. What a challenge. I am deep in thought. For once, I don't envy James. We had chosen an isolated place by the beach for our little get-together. I look around. No soul is in sight, only the wide, wild sea, shimmering in the distance like a piece of glass struck by a million sunrays. Carol isn't through yet.

"Having an alternative lifestyle doesn't make me less of a human being," she says. It doesn't make me evil. It just makes me me. No one will even try to understand. Why don't you two leave me alone? Leave me alone."

"You will have to calm down Carol," I say, a little quake to my voice.

"Keep out," Carol rounds on me. "What do you know about this?"

"James," she says, "if you don't want me in your house, I'll go quietly away. But please spare my children. The knowledge of what I'm will hurt them. Spare my poor parents. I love them so much to bring them pain. I know I've failed all of you, but then this is my life. "

"With you I've never felt like a man," James blurts out. "With you I've never gotten the pleasure of sexual satisfaction. Meanwhile, you have been doling it out-"

"At least, it wasn't to a man," I say, my counsel seeming insufficient. I hated myself.

"You should have told me, Caroline. Perhaps- perhaps we would still have gotten married."

"You are a good man, James, you are. But you would have been more than a saint to agree to marry a self-confessed lesbian. It would have been cruel to ask that of you. And I couldn't be cruel to you. You are such a nice person."

Carol blows her nose noisily, beginning to sob.

"You know James, I'm not ashamed," she says in-between sobs. "I didn't create myself. I tried loving the male body, your body. I tried loving the ripples of muscles on your arms, chest, legs and stomach. I tried loving your smell. But it was no use. The feel of your hands upon my skin made me sick. Instead of being wet and warm at the thought of your body against mine at night, I cringed. I dried up. We could never meet without you sustaining bruises. You once said I was frigid. Remember I did not argue with you then? How could I? This body of mine! These senses of mine! I've since hated them for being different. For choosing differently. You think it is easy being different? You think being different is my choice?"

All the while Carol is talking, my head is bowed; my jaw rests against my chest.

I can't exactly recall how the afternoon ended. Or rather, the thing that I remember most vividly about that afternoon is of walking home with my tail between my legs, like a frightened puppy. James and I had gone out with the intention of shaming Carol. Instead, our eyelids had been prised wide apart. Our eyes were shined.

But James was a man. Here was Africa. Not fucking Europe or America where one did as it pleased him. How dare Carol? James protested. Not that I blamed him. He began to stay away from home. He arranged one business trip after another, whined endlessly about how unfair life was, and took to making such dark allusions as, 'One might as well chose one very fine day and hang oneself.'

"She has never been with another man and that is something," I say one day as we sit brooding, like two school kids awaiting punishment. "Besides, she is quite discreet. She respects your feelings."

James, with jaws apart gapes at me. I ignore him and continue:

"Think of what will happen to your kids if you let the rope slip."

But this was asking too much from James. Or, from any man for that matter. The James I knew - the James I used to know - was one who even when at his wits' end kept a bold face. But, this problem of finding his wife in such an uncompromising situation. It was a huge wave.

He continued to stay out late and arranged more travels. His office became his home. He dressed poorly, ate poorly, lost weight. He drank more coffee. Neat. And he drank more beer. And gin and brandy and whisky too. He became depressed. Then he made a diplomatic blunder. The French country he was serving was embarrassed. They threw him out, appointed a new Charge de Affair. James's life disintegrated. I knew it would not be long before his family went to ruin. I stopped going to his house. Or, visiting him in his office. I was afraid.

Months have since passed.

I don't know how he is faring. The shame. It kills me, being of no use to him, like a loose tooth. Yes, a loose tooth. That is what I am, a loose tooth. James had been good to me. With his diplomatic connections, I had done myself well; padded myself real easy. I still maintain the contacts he gave me. I wish I could do something to halt the rot he and his family are experiencing. But I am a loose tooth, of no use. I might as well choose a fine day and...Or better still, slink away somewhere, never to be seen again.

I remember Syl and other stories

6

whim of the gods

(i)

Enugu: Eastern Nigeria. (8.07 a.m.)
The heavens, since the day dawned was as black as a ripe *ube* (pear), arousing in one the desire for that delicious combination of *oka* (maize-roast or boiled) and *ube* whose season was in full swing. Unable to make up their minds whether it was day or not, the chickens chipped noisily and contentedly away in their pen.

The rain, when it came poured down, as if with vengeance, to undo everything the welcome sun of August break had put in place since it stole the show a week ago. It pounded the old, corrugated zinc roof with vehemence, punishing it for frolicking with the sun. In solidarity, and with greater ferocity, the wind, which accompanied it threatened to bring down the foundations of the old, red mud kitchen.

Ugonna paid the elements no attention. For all she cared, they could tear through the roof of the kitchen. As if challenged by her indifference, the rain pounded harder, the accompanying thunder flashing and rumbling angrily. She was seated on a low, kitchen stool, enjoying her tasty breakfast of *Ede* (cocoa-yam) and peppered, fresh palm oil, graciously savouring the burning tang of the fresh green pepper. One thing was certain though: her date with Zubi that morning was as good as cancelled. She knew the rain would last for at least three good hours. But she was too exhilarated to mind. After three months of wasting away at home, she would be going back to school.

Just yesterday evening, she had heard the announcement on the radio: the Federal government had finally announced the re-opening of all universities and higher institutions across the nation. She recalled the broadcaster's low drone: "All students are to go back to school immediately and are expected to be of good behaviour." She was especially relieved that the government had promulgated a new decree, banning all forms of cult activities on campuses. It remained to be seen whether they would be able to effect the decree.

During these past three months, Ugonna had paid strict attention to her tiny World receiver, hoping not to miss the news about the re-opening of the universities. Having struck a commensal relationship with the vendor on the next street, she had read all the daily newspapers too. She dreaded a repetition of last year: then she was in 300 level. She had failed to learn of the re-opening of her school, the University of Nigeria, Nsukka, after a six-month closure due to secret cult activities.

She had ended up missing her papers during that second semester examination. It took the combined efforts of the Student Union president, Frank Alozie, and her dean, Professor Ben Ndudi, who incidentally was her Course Adviser, to get the senate to allow her a complete re-sit. Thank goodness she did not have to repeat that academic session. It would have been too painful. Already, she had spent six years for a four-year programme, due to the constant shutting down of her university.

Ugonna's only regret as she mentally prepared to go back to her school was Zubi: she would miss him. Her chest constricted with affection, and she elicited a deep sigh. Balancing her head on her left palm, with elbow rested on a kitchen table, she closed her eyes: if not for these constant interruptions of academic work, by now she would have graduated as an accountant and making good money, in a position to help her *mma* carry the burden of raising her younger brothers.

She would also have gotten married to Zubi —that dependable, ebony-black *angel* who had stood by her since the time her father got buried alive in the coalmines of Enugu, years ago. A migrant worker, Ugonna's father had come from Aba, away from the harrowing economic depression that engulfed that part of Eastern Nigeria immediately after the Nigerian-Biafran civil war in 1970.

Enugu, meaning 'hill top' had rich deposits of coal within its rocky hills. After the war, it had fared better than other parts of the East, attracting a large number of migrant workers from within and outside Nigeria. Like the other migrants, Ugonna's father had come to work the bowels of the hills. There, like large earthworms, they burrowed, digging until sunset, in search of the black mineral most came to believe was rightfully coloured black by the gods, and knowingly buried deep within the earth where it rightly belonged, for it was devilish.

She had been fifteen, and in her penultimate year at Girls' High School, Enugu, when her father died. She still remembered that day clearly, as if it were yesterday: they had done the compulsory morning devotion at the family altar, before the Holy Mary, ever Virgin. Each of them, including her two little brothers had, as was usual for Saturdays, recited ten 'Hail Marys', and five 'Our Fathers'. After breakfast (which he normally took at the mines on week days, because he had to leave much earlier), he had set out for the mines with his lunch pack, slung over his miner's broad and powerful shoulders. He was as fit as a fiddle. Next time she saw him was three days later when he was extracted from under the earth, dead, and in an advanced stage of decomposition.

Ugonna thought she would die then. She had been so attached to her father, a fact which engendered tension between her parents. It was Zubi who had stood by her side and helped her recover from the shock and, over the years, gradually heal.

Zubi, blacker than the deadly coal, was built like a prize-fighter. He exuded energy. His gentle manners (which contrasted with his physique), when coupled with his rasping singsong voice would melt mighty chunks of Olumo rock. He lived in the neighbourhood but was always away, attending University at Zaria, a town in one of Nigeria's northern states. He wanted to become an engineer. It was while the neighbourhood people came to pay condolences to her family that she had first set eyes on him. He too had come to commiserate with the bereaved family.

After everything, when the last visitor had come and gone, Zubi remained. He had stayed with the family ever since. He quickly became her new father, playing the role to perfection. He allayed her fears, and was always there to rock her to sleep in his strong, capable arms. His smiling coalface, which announced his intense white teeth like nothing else, and his fully bearded jaw, left her giddy with confidence. She didn't know how he managed it, but Zubi was always there, university or not.

And now, seven years after his graduation, they were going to get married. They would live in Enugu. Zubi worked in Enugu, managing one of his father's numerous engineering outfits. Despite her poor background as the first daughter of a dead and poor immigrant coal miner, Zubi's family, gentle souls, had approved their impending union. It was not such a difficult decision: both families were Roman Catholics.

Suddenly, the rumbling thunder clapped violently, shaking her out of her lengthy reverie. Ugonna sighed. Slowly, she opened her eyes. To accustom them to the brightening weather, she massaged them tenderly with the thumb and middle finger of her left hand, least likely to be contaminated with pepper. She watched tens of tiny black ants at work, busily dragging fragments of palm oil-stained cocoa yam in threes to their homes through numerous pin-like holes on the red earth floor and her heart glowed: graduation was only three months away. Her dreams would soon come true.

Yet, deep within her subconscious, she had this uncanny feeling which left her melancholic. It had been with her since she woke up: maybe it is because of the horrible dream I had last night, which made me wet myself, she thought. In the dream, she had gone to pick *ero* (mushroom) for the family soup. She had suddenly found herself in the centre of the forest, face to face with a man-eating, lion-like monster. A man (she thought he looked familiar) had appeared out of nowhere to save her, just as the monster rushed to devour her. With her screams stuck in her throat, she had woken as her saviour and the monster locked horns in a do or die battle.

Ugonna couldn't quite place the dream, and fingered the tiny, golden crucifix - Zubi's first gift- on her slender neck. She again heard Zubi's cooing voice as he clasped the chain: it will guide you when I am not there, though I will always be around you, never more than a breath away.

She believed him: hadn't he proven his steadfastness all these years beyond reasonable doubt?

Still fingering the crucifix, she mouthed one Hail Mary.

** **

Two weeks later. University of Nigeria, Nsukka: Eastern Nigeria.

Ugonna arrived at campus looking as exquisite as ever. Though she didn't own much, she used what little she had to their fullest advantage. A cheap skirt that would look drab on any other girl looked smashing on her. Having inherited a dazzling, fair complexion from her paternal lineage, she was convinced she didn't need make-up. And never wore any.

Finely boned, she commanded a second glance from everybody. Males adored her and females envied her the attention she received from the males that mattered on campus. What made Ugonna particularly attractive was her petit nature. She looked so vulnerable in that her silky, slippery walk, which had become her very signature on campus. Every man wanted to own her, so as to keep her from harm's way. More than anyone else, Walter wanted her.

Walter had wanted her from the first day he set eyes on her, six years ago. Walter was an enigma. He was in his fifth year in the Medical School. Nobody ever saw Walter studying -either in his room or in any lecture theatre. Students could count how many times they had seen him receiving lectures. Course mates could also count how many times they had seen him at *Clinicals*. But Walter had never failed a single exam. He had never missed one either, though surprisingly, he never spent more than thirty minutes for a three-hour paper. Rumours had it that what he puts down on his scripts were only his name and matriculation number, and diagrams of maybe an amputated leg, or a broken arm, or a dead man, or a

whim of the gods

disfigured child, whichever caught his fancy. No matter what diagram he chose to draw, one thing was true: he scored something above a B minus. Very few women could resist Walter. He was too rich and too handsome. He even had royal blood. If the money and blue blood didn't get them -though they invariably did- his sweetness did, for if there was any sweet, handsome young man, it was Walter! He could compete with the gods …that Walter! That Ugonna failed to respond to his charms was therefore mind-boggling, especially knowing she was from a poor background.

He had bought her everything there was to buy for a woman. He wasn't sure what she did with the expensive Yves St. Laurent clothes, Giorgio Armani perfumes and other designer wears. Perhaps she re-sold them: not that he minded. On setting eyes on her now, after these months of missing her, he tried a *toasting* angle he had since overlooked: who knows, he told himself.

"Look baby, I will take you anywhere, any place if only you agree to be mine."

Yellow cheeks dimpled, deep enough to poke the small finger into. That soothing voice that drives him bunkers:

"Anywhere is no where."

"London, I mean London."

His heart raced.

Small, even, brilliant, white teeth sparkled against the midday sun: Ugonna was like that. It was her philosophy to shower everyone with her endearing smile, especially in a big university campus like hers where you weren't sure who was who. The fellow you acted cool towards may have affiliations in one campus cult or another. And may some day come to extract vengeance for perceived injustices. That explained why she had been very tactful in disposing of the gifts Walter bombarded her with every now and then.

She smiled on.

Patiently, Walter waited.

Time passed.

The pressure of the waiting was punishment for Walter. At last, he could take it no more and cried:

"Baaaaaby anywhere …the moon, aaaanywhere …London!"

Ugonna's voice rang out:

"Really…?"

For Walter, this was nothing but a 'YES'.

** **

75

"I got her...I got her..." Walter exploded, no sooner than he stepped into the noisy bar where he knew he was sure to find members of his gang. They took a break from their wet bottles of Gulder and heavy wraps of billowing, crackling *wee-wee* (marijuana) and gaped.

"Who?...Got who?" someone asked.

"My woman...my heartthrob. That sweet angel, Uuuu...Uuuu ...Uuuu-"

"Ugonna," someone completed for him.

"Yes. Ugonna!"

A deep sigh pervaded the gang.

Silence.

A snort: "I wonder how much you have thrown to the dogs this time."

"Piss off man. It's none of your business."

"Never said it was."

"You might as well know that she didn't take a dime from me," Walter announced proudly. "Not a dime, you hear me, nosy bastards. She is not one of those if you must know. She is *my* woman, very well brought up."

Lifted Gulder bottles found their ways back to the tables, banging; while inhaled puffs of bluish-white smoke were quickly exhaled, followed by the eruption of deep, racking coughs, soon suppressed with generous swigs from beer bottles. Why, no girl on campus ever, ever said a 'yes' without, like the IMF and World Bank, laying down rigorous provisos. Their motto was: *'money for hand, back for ground'.*

Walter knew he had his friends seething with envy, and basked and trotted in the spine-tingling feeling and strength the knowledge gave him.

"You must have promised her something, at least," one pal said as the bunch recovered from their shock.

"I did promise her something, though."

A smile, suddenly breaking out here, like the sun, peeking out of the cloudy sky on a wet unpromising morning. A slight cough there. Curious glances everywhere.

Another pal: "Tell us, what exactly did you promise *your* woman?"

"What I promised her is my business."

"Eh, come on, man. Be a dude and come clean. After all, we will eventually know."

"Let's say it's a secret."

"All her friends already know about the damned secret by now, don't you think?" someone suggested cleverly.

The bunch waited patiently while Walter chewed the idea with his mind's teeth, turning the paste around carefully with his mind's tongue.

They knew it must be something substantial: whatever had made that pretty, stubborn 'home grown babe' change her mind without demanding compensation. It had been centuries since the duo began playing their hide and seek game.

"I promised to take her to London."

Dead silence!

The former faint squeaking of the ceiling fan as it circled lazily now became overpoweringly loud, like a faulty helicopter's propeller. And then, without warning, the bar erupted as shrill whistling rent the air, drowning the fan's squeaky noise. Some of Walter's pals held their heads, shaking it vigorously, while others closed their eyes and taxed their brains in attempts to meditate on the piece of wondrous news: high concentration of alcohol, nicotine and cannabinol made the task impracticable.

"You did what?" It was a troubled, small voice. Someone had miraculously recovered from the trauma the information wrecked. His recovery set the pace, as the others around the long table gradually came to, each scrutinizing Walter more closely.

"Yes, I did. I promised her."

"A mere bitch?"

"Don't call her a bitch, man," Walter thundered. "She is my *shit.* You hear me, my *shit.*"

And the matter was closed.

** **

To fulfil his promise, Walter sent a photographer pal after Ugonna. The clandestine job was a piece of cake: thanks to digital technology. With the passport picture the photographer handed over, Walter obtained Ugonna an international passport, after forging her simple signature. He then had a genuine multiple entry British visa issued into the passport. All these accomplishments took him less than a month …That Walter, there was simply nothing beyond him, except maybe assuming the title, 'Pope John Paul'. Even that…

He had once boasted to his inner caucus that if he wanted, he could unsit the vice-chancellor! Very few doubted him. Such was the degree of muscles he wielded. What left members of his gang confounded, however, was why he had failed to win the approval of that petit broad, Ugonna.

Now that too was settled.

Another feather to his cap.

** **

The parcel came as Ugonna was exiting Auditorium II, having just ended STAT 412, a course she didn't particularly like. But she wasn't expecting anything from Zubi...Suspicious, she bid the courier wait as she rushed to the ladies. As soon as the door clicked shut, she ripped open the brown envelope, and the green passport fell out.

Tentatively, she picked it up:

Perhaps Zubi had...Why not make sure? Here was a note... Not Zubi's writing_

She turned over the envelope: Of course, not Zubi's writing_ Who could this be?

Her hands shook as she opened the note and read:

'The passport, my sweetheart...'

WHAT?

'...Your visa...'

WHAT?

'...London...'

Her throat went dry as her hands vibrated. The passport flapped. And dropped. She recalled that exchange weeks back. And suddenly, anger seized her:

What guts? How dare he snap her photograph without her consent? Her signature...forged, he probably went to Admin to rape her file... Who did he think he was?

Ugonna grabbed the passport. And with all the strength her slender hands could muster, she yanked off the picture and signature page: This more than anything else would tell him ...no, she needed to put it in black and white.

Opening her handbag, she drew out a jotter. And found a red pen.

** **

Ugonna had no regrets as she watched the courier's receding back. She told herself: philosophy or not, there comes a time when one MUST take a firm stand. Suddenly the whole thing seemed comical, and in spite of herself, she shook so hard with laughter that her eyes watered: oh, he was such a baby, that Walter.

** **

Within minutes, Walter had his envelope back. Oh, you should have seen him. Imagine stepping on a rattler's sore tail. Or poking a hungry man with fire. What broke his heart, and shattered his ego the most was not the destroyed passport itself, but Ugonna's accompanying note, in neat handwriting, which read:

'Prince Walter Ezeh,

"Please cease worrying yourself with thoughts of me. You will never have a place in my heart. I belong to another."

Ugonna Anaeke.'

Walter's pals were most sympathetic.

"Women," someone hissed after reading the note and leafing through the destroyed passport. "With them, you never know."

Before the end of that day, more than twenty able-bodied, young men had trooped from all corners of the campus to read and re-read the note, and inspect and re-inspect the destroyed passport, as Walter lay comatose on his custom-built spring bed. For acknowledgement of lipped, but heartfelt sympathy from members of his gang, he merely nodded his head slowly, several times, not unlike a male agama in glorious colours. You would think he had suffered a severe stroke.

And exams were only a matter of weeks away. Ugonna would graduate and go unconquered. She wanted to make him, Walter, a laughing stock. That would be setting a bad example. It would not happen. *He would hit her.*

Like Walter feared, he was becoming a laughing stock. His friends now snickered behind his back. That evening, he overheard a rather disturbing discussion as he went to use the loo.

"I think I need something for my woman."

"Something like what?"

"Something special, you know..."

"Like what?"

"Like an International Passport, complete with a Shengen visa. ...who knows, me and my babe might be needing to do a bit of globetrotting after our exams."

And the loo shook on its foundations as great rumbling sounds bounced back and forth against tiled walls and ceramic cisterns.

"Ha, ha, ha, hi, hi."

"Ho, ho, ho, ha, ha."

It was Willy and Josy.

Walter ground his teeth savagely and stumped back to his room, nature's call forgotten! Day in, day out, as he lay condemning his liver with his Remy Martin, roasting his lungs with his *wee-wee*, and contemplating events, he would re-affirm his vow of, *I will hit her!*

In between his fury, his brain would creak: who is this another that she belongs to? Well, he will have her corpse.

** **

A week later.

Standard cult procedure dictated that, irrespective of who moved it, all motions for hits be fully debated. An uncontested hit was null and void. That was how the *Mongoose Confraternity* operated.

And so, Walter hissed his motion:

"I want that bitch hit."

He was menacing. For the first time in a long, long while he was sober, and as serious as a church. All watching and listening knew that he was in full control of his faculties.

To Walter's advantage, Josy came in furiously.

"Let her be. She is too pretty to die."

And the debate was in full swing.

Mighty, hairy chests rose and fell rhythmically, as if to the beating of the *Igbo* traditional drum, *Udu.* Faces distorted with scars of different tints and lengths twitched. Broad nostrils flared, blasting hot air. Giant biceps contracted and relaxed as damp fists were clenched, unclenched and re-clenched.

"She should not be allowed to set a bad example on campus," somebody snarled, siding with Walter.

"She doesn't know *what* he is. So she *is* innocent," came another defence.

It was Willy.

Walter took a deep breath and smiled sardonically: Nobody crosses Walter and lives to tell the tale. Like a lion, I will stalk and maul these two pigs when all this is over.

"Why doesn't the bitch want to be fucked by a real man?" came a hiss from somewhere in the now smoke filled room. "She is only a piece of pussy, isn't she, guys? Common, let's stick with our *King Crown.*"

Walter knew this was the time to exercise *his* powers.

"Let's ballot. That's what the constitution says."

Walter had single-handedly written that constitution. That was three years ago when he was elected *King Crown* (national leader of the *Mongoose Confraternity*) at a Congress in the Ekenwan Campus of the University of Benin, Mid-western Nigeria. Used to the backstabbing and deadly hypocrisy in his father's royal court, he had made sure the

80

constitution read, 'Open ballot'. Though when it suited him, 'Open ballot' translated to 'Secret ballot'. He always knew what arguments to submit.
'Clemento?' –Let's hit her.
'Angelo?' –She goes down.
'Ogadinma?' –Down with her.
'Nwaokorie?' –Let's fuck her.
'Brazil?' —Let her die.
'Aso Rock?' –She must fall.
'Son of Man?' – The Last Supper ...Feed her and she will never hunger again!
...And the balloting went on.
Final count: twenty for, none against!
No one voted against the King Crown. Not in an Open ballot anyway. As soon as the decision was safely in the bag, words were rushed out to a unanimous, but carefully selected sister university. A chosen few made this selection: to avoid any danger of leakage.
Obafemi Awolowo University, Ile-Ife, Western Nigeria was chosen.
They would provide Ugonna's nemesis!

(ii)

Next day. Obafemi Awolowo University, Ile-Ife: Western Nigeria. (3.23 p.m.)
Like a tightly compressed spring, Lekan sprang as soon as the large, calloused hands, rougher than sandpaper, alighted softly on his wide shoulder. The intruder's heart hopped frantically to his mouth as he took a hasty step back.
Lekan had stolen to Agric Lecture room 203 in an attempt to catch up with his coursework, left unattended since school reopened. He had dozed into a troubled sleep in the process. As his eyes cleared, he found himself staring into Johnny's hard, sneaky eyes, made bloodshot by the cheap, illicit gin, *'Push me I push you.'*
Lekan, face clouded with resentment, wrinkled his nose in disgust and waited, every muscle in his athletic body tautly attentive. In answer to the question, scribbled on his firmly knotted brow, Johnny issued forth a controlled, gruffly grunt:
"You have been chosen as the faithful for another hit. You are to report to headquarters for briefing. *He* says to tell you time is running out."
Smiling sheepishly and baring nicotine-stained, shovel-like teeth, Johnny punched his clenched right fist into the palm of his left hand (the *Mongoose* code!) after casting quick glances left and right to make sure he

81

wasn't being spied.

"See ya later."

And Johnny disappeared into thin air like a whiff of smoke, leaving behind a sickening stench. Lekan dragged in a bag of air, and then exhaled deeply. Shutting his eyes tightly, he shook his head vigorously for long seconds, as if doing so would convince him that he had been dreaming, or make the reality of what he had just heard go quietly away. When nothing happened, he emitted a deep, deep sigh: why him, so soon again?

But he didn't make the decisions. He was committed to the cause ...had been for the past five years. In that time, he had thought of abandoning the *Mongoose* secret cult and running away. But more than anyone else, he knew it was hopeless to try. The very idea itself was laughable, for the *Mongoose* secret cult was no 'Boys' Scout' or 'Man-o-war'. Nobody joined and left when he or she felt like it. Plus, that would mean forfeiting his university education.

Angry with himself, Lekan straightened up, revealing his full six and half feet, which boasted a well shaped head seated deftly atop a solid, solid neck. He would probably have been much shorter if not for the neck endowment. As he began to put his books away, he allowed his mind to drift back to that time when it all started.

** **

He had spent only three months at the Obafemi Awolowo University, full of zest and high hopes. He was determined to succeed, if only to prove his mum wrong. It was during a belated welcome party organized for fresh law students that *they* had first made contact with him. He had been on his way to his hostel, deep in thought about an impending philosophy test, which, according to the lecturer, 'would be tougher than steel'.

Suddenly, the lanky guy had stopped him and smiled amiably:

"Hello, my name is St. Iyke. I saw you at the orientation. Had fun?"

Without waiting for a reply, this St. Iyke carried on: "It's not easy here, you know. But you will get along fine. Just as long as you belong to the right group, that is."

Watching St. Iyke keenly, Lekan said nothing.

"I am in my third year, studying law too. Should you need anything, feel free to check me out. I will be very glad to help."

St. Iyke smiled his amiable smile again, setting Lekan at ease.

"I reside at Fajuyi Hall, room 303," St. Iyke revealed.

Before taking his leave, he extended an invitation to Lekan for a little get-together his guys were stringing together for new friends.

"It will be fun," he assured. "Next week Friday, why not pop in?"

For the first time, Lekan smiled.

"The party will help you unwind. You will meet a lot of *jambites* like you from other faculties. And you will make new pals who will help you watch your back."

That little get-together was what ended up as an introduction to the *Mongoose Confraternity*, the most potent secret cult in Obafemi Awolowo University, with affiliations in all other campuses across Nigeria.

Once you were introduced, there was no going back. Initiation, which involved blood rituals and hunting down live cobras, was only a matter of weeks from the date of the first introductory meeting. Before extending an invitation for anyone to come meet new friends cum back watchers, that person had been followed for several weeks, even months, his background studied and carefully documented.

The mandate of the *'Brotherhood,'* as members preferred to call it, was to protect one another from intimidation, harassment, and the so-called injustices from so-called sadist lecturers. Their motto, *'an arm for an arm'* meant that like the mongoose, they extracted vengeance for any wrong done to them by any cobra (person), and would go to any length to ensure this.

For security reasons, it was standard procedure for an individual, or a troop from one university (on invitation only) to travel thousands of kilometres to another to extract a particular payback or *'hit.'* But once in a while, under the most astringent checks, quick reprisals on offenders were deftly planned and executed internally, especially if the offenders were members of other campus cults, who should have known better than cross members of the deadly *Mongoose.* This often led to bloody clashes where innocent students were maimed or killed.

It was on account of one of these killings that high institutions across the country were shut down for nearly three months, and had only recently resumed. A final year Literature student at the Bayero University, Kano, Northern Nigeria had had his eyes gouged out with a hot prong, and his genitalia severed. An autopsy had revealed where the severed genitalia was: in his stomach. It had been diced and cooked medium-rare.

** **

The last five years had seen Lekan traversing nearly all universities in Nigeria, extracting vengeance on behalf of his *Brotherhood.* What he had

83

to show for these clandestine missions were several meetings with his Faculty Officer. The last one, at the beginning of the semester, was terse and straight to the point. He recalled walking into the FO's well-furnished office on jelly legs:

"Mr. Lekan Aremu?"

A slow nod.

"Well, I am calling you for the same reason I have called you severally, remember?"

Another nod. Slower than the first.

"Five years you have been in this faculty, and still in part two. Well, this is your last warning. If you don't meet the minimum GPA at the end of this semester to move you to part three, the faculty would have no other option but to kindly advise you to withdraw. Do you understand me?"

Several nods. Each as slow as painful death.

"It shouldn't be a difficult task. From your first year result before me here, I am of the impression that if you disciplined yourself, you will yet make it."

Lekan knew this was true! But could he ever settle down? What with all these assignments from the *Brotherhood.*

"Here is a letter from this office with regard to our discussion today."

Lekan accepted the letter with his right hand. The FO failed to notice the tremor, which rattled the paper, ever so slightly.

If only the shame of imminent rustication was where his pains ended. But it wasn't. Three years ago, during a *hit* that went sour at the Imo State University, Eastern Nigeria, he had come out scarred. That particular experience still haunts him.

True, the wound had healed, but he was now a marked man, with his left hand permanently sheltered in his pocket or under his shirt. What was more? His high hopes of becoming a renowned lawyer had since slipped away. His mum would say she was right: he would end up a bum, like his father.

Lekan had never known his father!

And he had always wanted to prove himself. The *Mongoose Confraternity* had shown instant appreciation of his stature, assuaging his self-esteem. He felt needed and useful, unlike the scumbag, his mother, forever comparing him with his father, always made him believe he was.

How time had changed all that. He should have known better than allow the sly, smooth talking St. Iyke to hoodwink him years ago. But how could he have known?

Like a millstone around his neck, he felt the burden of his naivety daily.

** **

As Lekan's sweat splattered on his open notebooks, and the blue ink began to run, reminding him of a chromatography experiment in secondary school when he attempted chemistry, he was hauled back from his disturbing reverie. Wiping the sweat from his face, forearm and books, he packed up with lightning speed. Hurriedly, he walked out of the empty lecture room: nobody kept a *Crown* (the name by which local Mongoose leaders were known) waiting.

The Crown wasted no time with pleasantries.

"You are going to Nsukka now."

An imperceptible twitch, and Lekan's eyes narrowed into slits. His clammy left hand, safely out of sight, fisted and un-fisted. His Adam's apple bobbed and danced, like a plastic can tossed about by angry waves.

"You know how to get there, don't you?"

Without waiting for answer, the Crown continued in his sombre voice, like the Campus Priest he was:

"You will receive further instructions at Nsukka."

A thick, brown envelope exchanged hands.

"Your transport allowance. I would have briefed you fully, but I have confessions to attend to. My parishioners are waiting. Good luck."

The truth was that the Priest felt uneasy, alone with his formidable hit man. A seminarian who gained admission to study Philosophy and Religious Studies at Ile-Ife, Fr. Badmus Adeniran had been at his duty post as the Crown of Obafemi Awolowo University since graduation ten years ago.

** **

An hour later, Lekan boarded a luxurious bus at the motor park in town; it would be an all night trip. Immediately after, a special call was made from Ile-Ife, using a public booth. The idea of tailing Lekan from the campus had not been palatable, for nobody had the know how to stick successfully to his tail. So the caller had been at the motor park a full hour before Lekan's arrival, stowed away in a squalid bar, with an uninterrupted view of the motor park.

The call, arriving at the telecom switchboard at Nsukka, was spontaneously rooted to its recipient at the university. The recipient,

85

grunting and coughing short, dry coughs after a sustained drag on a heavy wrap of *wee-wee*, recognized the incoming code on his Nokia handset and sprang from his bed as if doused with ice water.

He composed his voice, as befitted a king.

"Talk to me!" he snapped.

"The good has been dispatched."

"Ughhh?..."

"Reporting that the good is on its way."

"When will I take delivery?"

"First thing tomorrow morning."

"No fuck ups..."

Silence.

"I said no fuck ups..."

The silence, transmitted across 600km by radio waves deepened.

"I said no fucking fuck ups..."

The voice had lost its composure now.

"Mighty-Ife-does-not-f-u-c-k-u-p *King Crown*," was reverently spat at him.

Tugging furiously at his moustache, usually well groomed with intense care, but terribly dishevelled these days, Walter's eyes radiated thermal energy: Mighty Ife does not fuck up, yes, but what the heck? Who was this prick on the other end anyway? Didn't he know who he was speaking to?

His hands trembled.

He cast his red eyes about.

His pack was out: just as well!

And he began to sweat: fuck!

The caller at the other end waited patiently.

Again the King Crown composed his voice: it bore no iota of remorse.

"How do I know him?"

With grinding accuracy, the caller relayed Lekan's brute description.

And the phone died ...in his ear, just as he ended his description. Hurt, Johnny made a mental note to include both insults in his report to his Priest.

** **

Next day: University of Nigeria, Nsukka, Eastern Nigeria (6.01 am)
It was a chilly morning. Rough, whistling wind ruffled Lekan's brown gabardine trousers angrily, blowing dust into his face. He tasted grit and cursed. As he bent down to re-lace his black boots, which he had loosened in the crowded, luxurious bus, the aroma of *akara* (bean cakes) frying

nearby caught his broad, strong nostrils. Maybe he should have breakfast. He had eaten nothing for nearly eighteen hours. It was always like this. Then his trained instincts bade him that he had company: *They* were there. Breakfast was shelved until further notice.

Since five o'clock his *cousins* had been at the motor park, just outside the university's main gate, painstakingly scrutinizing every arriving passenger amid the cacophony of noise. The description fitted. Yet they waited for the diagnostic sign. Several seconds rushed by. And in a flash, Lekan's left hand zapped out of the pocket of his grey moccasin windbreaker to scratch his left ear lobe.

The ring and middle fingers were missing!

** **

This was going to be Lekan's first job at the University of Nigeria. Careful reading had taught him all there was to know about the campus except the topography. But no need to worry. His cousins would teach him all there was to know. They would also educate him about his quarry, on whom they already had a large dossier. After their exposé, they would let him tail her for several days.

Finally, they would cut him loose.

This of course, was after the loosening-up ritual.

This ritual involved *catching* three full-grown cobras with bare hands. He would then de-venom and parade them for inspection before skinning and dumping them, whole, into a steaming pot of *wee-wee* pepper soup! The ritual would climax when he ate the three cobras heads (his share), and picked his teeth with their fangs!

It was all in the book.

Lekan didn't mind!

He was a skilled *Naja* catcher. Like Ile-Ife, Nsukka had plenty of them and more to spare. All his cousins had to do was point him in the right direction. He preferred 'fighting *Najas*' to 'running *Najas*'. You never knew where a running *Naja* would lead you. He still shudders at a certain memory: once, while chasing an old and tired *Naja* which could hardly spit, he had found himself right in a *Naja* den, confronted by five-angry cobras! Only his dexterity had saved him.

When in a new territory, Lekan listened carefully to instructions, absorbing every detail, like a sponge. His survival on the field, he knew, depended on the degree of finer details he was able to store. For lack of this foresight, several of his colleagues had been nailed on missions.

Against popular opinion, alcohol and *marijuana* were potent killers on the job. Lekan knew this and avoided them like the plague. And he left no trail, making him the most sought for *Mongoose* hit man on campus.

Ile-Ife was very proud to have him.

(iii)

Two weeks later. Thursday.
7.05pm
Ugonna was a conscientious student, and was already at her corner at Education Lecture Room 2. She wanted to better her fiancé, Zubi, who had graduated with a second-class lower. She sometimes wondered why he hadn't done better. As far as she knew, he was quite brilliant. And so she burnt her candles on both ends as she prepared for her final exams. It was her usual manner to leave class late, trudging the dark sidewalks alone. You could call her a loner. Though she sometimes felt better if fellow students were around on the way back to the hostel.

9.37 pm
A flickering candlelight cast coarse, grotesque images of five hooded men in boots on the whitewashed wall of a one-room, apartment. Located off campus, the room was small, with one tiny, gauzed window. Damp, it had the characteristic cold smell of cassava mould. A six-spring bed sat in the centre. A windbreaker hung on a rusted six-inch nail stabbed into one wall. Business began after the foot shuffling had ceased, and heartbeats could be clearly heard.

"Doing the job tonight...?"

A slow nod. Silence.

"No mistakes..."

Pressurized silence.

"I said, no mistakes..."

A deep, deep swallow: "I-don't-make-mistakes."

Chests rose and fell.

Time passed.

"Good luck then."

"I-don't-need-luck."

Few men shook Walter's liver. Lekan belonged to that regal group. His body shook with a slight tremor. He hoped nobody noticed.

Lekan missed nothing.

"Very well, then," Walter said, and walked out of the apartment, his three bodyguards on his heels. Outside, a flash of light on the solid gold chronometer, resting on his hairy, light-skinned hand as someone lit a cigarette, told him the time: 9.45pm.

Lekan detested Walter: Why, the fellow was too arrogant. And the girl didn't deserve to die. Not for him. The fart! He recalled Walter's instruction when he first arrived: you must make her suffer. And totally unrecognisable?

Lekan would have loved it to be a neat job. Suffocation by poison gas. But his policy was to obey instruction to the *letter*. He would make her unrecognisable. It would be easy. Girls were always easy. And then he would ask that he be left alone, at least for a while. He could recommend others. He knew more than a dozen, equally competent guys. They would understand if he told them about the threat of expulsion.

10.09pm
Ever so suspicious of fate's funny hand in shaping events, Lekan would not give in to suppositions. It bred error. He strolled into campus: just to make sure the girl was where he knew she would be. He felt sorry for her. She was very beautiful. They said she was pompous. She didn't act pompous, in his candid opinion. Why was he getting involved? Christ! It was unhealthy to get involved with one's victims. Shit! He didn't understand himself anymore.

Muttering obscenities, he licked his dry lips, glancing over his shoulders. He hoped he was not being followed. He walked into the night, his head tilted to a sloppy angle. He now represented misery and death. He hadn't planned it this way. Through him, numerous individuals had been sent to early graves. Through him, families have suffered untold agonies. Because of inconsequential misunderstandings and bickering bred by peer pressures. It was costing him his education. And his life. The relatives of those victims... how were they faring? He was sure they were terribly distraught- by his own hands! Bringing out his left hand, he surveyed the scars and the three remaining fingers briefly. They looked forlorn. He rushed them back to safety: *Nooooooo!*

** **

10.16pm
A new visitor arrived to join Ugonna's appointed nemesis, Lekan. This visitor was a *killer's killer*. He had his ears very close to the ground. He had ruled the entire *Buccaneer* confraternity in Nigeria for three good years from his base in Northern Nigeria. He was suave. But despite his politeness and simplicity, like a 4 x 4, he exuded solid power. He was a shiny black all

89

over. You could walk straight into him in the dark without knowing. Or he could steal up on you in the night and stand by your side for several minutes. If you were lucky, he let you go. Otherwise, you died!

Where Lekan was careful, precision was his hallmark. Being a precise killer, he had researched his adversary before setting foot on the campus. His research had yielded nothing, except that his adversary was a snake catcher, which wasn't much by way of bio data. The Mongoose were in their hundreds, and each, he knew from past experience, was **a** *'deadly nightshade.'*

'Never underestimate your enemy,' was his killer's slogan. Though he found out nothing personal and specific about his adversary's physical composition and attributes, at least he had taken the necessary precaution towards being alive. It was about doing the right thing. So instead of feeling despair, his spirit soared.

On arrival at Nsukka, he had registered with a false name at an out of the way motel. After making sure his BMW 7 Series was properly covered with tarpaulin, he had immediately made a call from the pay phone outside the motel premises. The people at the other end had been waiting for this call for nearly five hours, and relayed vital information. They were the same people who had invited him to this rendezvous. Only yesterday, they had sent him a DHL package. It read:

> "*Tracker,*
> *Target sinks tomorrow at anytime from midnight. A one-man party expected. Join the rendezvous. Call 9966543209 on arrival to confirm.*
> *The Moles.*

These contacts owed him their lives and were happy to supply this information freely. For six years now, he had oiled them to watch his back - just for a time like this. It had paid off: his instinct was always right. If his instincts were right again, the snake catcher wouldn't do the job the way he had pencilled it, for snake catchers never really revealed their *modus operandi.* Not even to their Crown Mongoose. They wouldn't ensnare themselves in their own trap. He wasted no time in identifying where the girl read.

Had he known his adversary, the *retired* Buccaneer would have breathed easier. Being a master killer, however, he knew ways to make amends for this major drawback, plus he had an overwhelming advantage: his presence was unknown.

Careful not to expose himself to peril, he selected a strategic position with an unobstructed view of the sidewalks. And lying down on the damp grass, he watched and waited patiently. He was a trained guerrilla fighter.

Not even the deadliest bite of the buzzing mosquitoes could make him swat.

12.11am
The Buccaneer saw what he had been watching out for. A tiny light ray piercing through a hibiscus flower on his far right was momentarily blocked for a split second as his adversary identified himself, assuming a crouching position, like a feline creature waiting to pounce. His heart missed several beats, as the muscles of his arms and legs flexed involuntarily. He gauged distances and estimated angles, like an engineer: *baaa...* He was a long way off. But he wasn't going to do anything about it for now. He wouldn't blow his delicate cover. Both killers had been trained to perceive and interpret, with precision, the tiniest night sounds and faintest smells, eliminating the obvious and zeroing in on the out of place. Ear lobes ached now as both listened intently, their nostrils flaring, tasting the cold, night air.

1.05am
Ugonna was completely alone. As always, the owls and bats frightened her as they flew from one tree to another, shrieking. This night they flapped violently, as if in protest of the impending rain. The nocturnal, torrential rain that signalled the end of the long rainy season had been threatening for the past three days. It looked likely this night. If she could only see the outline of the bats and owls and be sure they were the real things. One often heard stories of men flying at night. But her wish was never to be gratified, for the night was pitch dark and the sky devoid of stars.

As the trees waved and swayed to the violent urging of the wind, with branches taking the shape of demons' talons, she snuggled deeper and deeper into her sweater and clutched the tiny golden crucifix on her neck, invoking its protective powers as she began to chant: *'Hail Mary, full of grace...the Lord is with you...'*

And diligently, she walked on towards her hostel...and to her death.

1.07am
From their positions, both butchers saw her approach. One had seen her earlier as she stepped out of the lecture room. He had moved with her. While she moved northwards, he came in from his position in the west. He would have to intersect her at the exact point where the *Mongoose* awaited. It had to be with the speed of greased lightning. He strained his eyes, scanning for obstructions. Any along his path, slowing him for even a split second, would mean disaster, his mission irrevocably foiled. He could not

bear to think what it would mean to his life.

And she was moving too fast! He had not anticipated the bad weather, which was hastening her, for this was not her usual pace. He knew that too well. Hadn't he studied her until there was nothing left to study? Were he not a master of the jungle and a child of the night, he probably would have panicked. But like the killer leopard he was, he marched stealthily forward. He knew how to step lightly, like breeze, on dry twigs without snapping them. It was a deadly game of death...of winners take all. The other was going to pay dearly.

In his position, Lekan's heart ached for what he was about to do. He told himself he had no rights. He told himself *they* had no rights ...that it was all wrong ...the destruction, the pain, the hearts he was helping *them* ache. He would sooner take leave of them than go on this way. It had destroyed his life. But he was under oath. Oath he couldn't change because he didn't make the rules: if he didn't do it, somebody else would. And then several people would be dead because they would come after him. He wouldn't let them get him for nothing. But how many of them could he fight off? And for how long? But this girl ought not to die. *No!* His facial muscles twitched, and his left ear lobe itched. He scratched involuntarily, grinding his teeth, moaning over and over and over again, under heavy, warm breath, confused like a man with brain fever. But he must do it...to buy his freedom! After this, no more. He can't do it...he can't stop her death...only a miracle would save her now...her fate, his destiny...

This sudden dawn of fatalism gripped him with a cold hand, and he shivered violently. For the first time since he became a Mongoose hit man, Lekan felt his spirit dissolve, like salt in hot water.

1.09am
Did she hear something, like a heart beat? *'...Holy Mary, mother of God, pray for us sinners now...'*...It must be one of those dreadful owls. Or bats. *'...Pray for us sinners now and at the hour of our death...'* Ugonna increased her pace, not glancing back. Not that she could have seen anything if she did. The wind was howling wickedly now, and the whole place was in Stygian darkness, like the Gates of Hades.

1.11am
By the time he heard the gentle, gentle thin snap of a dry twig by his side, it was way too late. At first he didn't see anything, but then, still stooping and adjusting his black facial mask, he saw...and he was terribly, terribly terrified! Intently, both men peered into each other's eyes simultaneously. Despite the darkness, the Mongoose straining upwards from his stooping

position immediately recognized the Buccaneer bearing menacingly down on him. The outline of his shoulders, like the gates of a massive warehouse, was an unmistakable identity. Bile, bitter as brown ale, filled his mouth. He felt faint and hollow. Blood rushed to his brain and pounded away. He was too disadvantaged to do anything. He did not even try. For he knew what he knew: he had no chance in hell. As the razor sharp sickle sliced into his throat, like hot knife into butter, Lekan recalled vividly how he had encountered this man once and had two missing fingers as testimony. Everyone called him 'Darkness', for he was black all over, like the *devil* he was. But didn't he hear somewhere that the man was a practicing—? He couldn't recall what profession, as he humbly accepted his fate with a smile: he had won after all. This 'Darkness', killing him now, would have the girl's innocent blood on his hands, rather than he, Olalekan Aremu.

1.13am
As his quarry walked hurriedly past him, not a single hair on her light skin ruffled, Lekan died like a dog, without throwing a single punch. The last thing he noticed before sinking into oblivion was the splattering of what he knew would be a heavy rain. Dry season was here!

** **

Next day. 10.00 am.
It seemed for her, the day was filled with endless promises. Ugonna didn't know why or how, but thought the sun shone extra bright. It was warm and inviting. She felt light-headed too, nearly euphoric. Last night, the kind man in her dreams finally slaughtered the man-eating lion-like monster that had been terrorizing her nightly for weeks. She still couldn't make out his face. Could there be a connection with the charred body she heard students talking about? The idea shocked her: she didn't think so.

The entire student body had woken up, shocked, to find the unrecognisable corpse of a man lying on the grass, along one of the sidewalks. His face and chest and stomach were totally unrecognisable, the bones charred and the flesh completely eaten away. Curious looking oily liquid oozed out of the carcass. Students of analytical chemistry were quick to identify this curious liquid as a mixture of concentrated Sulphuric acid and Nitric acid. It was not long after that the authorities at the Department of Chemistry reported a break in at one of their laboratories.

"And you know," she had told one of her roommates when the news first broke out, "that was the very route I took on my way back from class last night. I wonder why that poor, innocent soul was murdered."

93

And she thought: I must never stay up so late anymore. I could have been the unfortunate victim of that acid attack. But again, Ugonna dismissed this silly thought emphatically: that wasn't her fate.

****

Enugu: Eastern Nigeria (8.00 am).
Zubi was in a bright, warm mood. He was impeccably dressed in a brilliant-white three-piece suit. He enjoyed beginning his days at the engineering outfit his father had bequeathed to him by 7.00 a.m. Today, however, he had come in a little late. He had had a late rendezvous at the university in Nsukka, an hour and forty-five minute drive away in his powerful BMW 7 Series. The success of that rendezvous far compensated for this morning's lateness.

a promise made...

One dry, windy, harmattan afternoon, an event, which was to alter Effuah's life forever, took place. She was getting set for the cameras, in preparation for an all-important shooting for the promotion of, *Ecstasy*, a new hair product. It was on this day that the man came calling, like the evil spirit who destroys a person on the day his life is sweetest. He came escorted by an old wiry woman who pushed his wheelchair. On arrival, the old woman, who was surprisingly strong for her age and frame, lifted him gingerly out of the wheelchair, depositing him in one of several soft executive cushions that adorned the visitors' waiting room.

The gatekeeper was furious. He had stepped out briefly, only to come back and find two total strangers whom he couldn't place inside his visitors' room. The man sprawled on one of the cushions, which he took great care wiping and polishing daily was dusty and sickly. The gatekeeper noted that he was crippled. And blind as well. Yellow pus oozed from both eyes. The gatekeeper opened the door and spat. He lifted the window blinds and tucked them neatly in one edge, letting in fresh air.

"What have you come here for?" he asked at length.

"I have come *for* the beauty queen," the crippled man said.

His voice was strong. It carried far and bore all the elements of déjà. The gatekeeper wasn't sure he had heard right, and repeated, this time sternly.

"What have you come here for?"

"The beauty queen," the blind cripple answered.

"The beauty queen, did you say?"

"Yes."

"Look dad, if it is money you want-"

"It is not money I want."

What would the blind man possibly want, the gatekeeper thought. Perhaps he was a beggar. But the gatekeeper knew all the beggars in town.

"Dad, come back tomorrow. Effuah has an important shooting today. The cameras are already rolling."

The gatekeeper unbuttoned his long sleeves at the wrist and folded them. Then he began pulling them above his elbows. Beggar or not; yellow pus or not, he was determined to carry the crippled, old, blind man shoulder high out of the waiting room. It was an unwelcome task, but he had no choice in the matter. If the cripple were looking for a place to relax-

"Pulling up your shirt sleeves will not achieve anything," the crippled, blind man said, interrupting the gatekeeper's train of thoughts. "Just call her. Tell her there is someone here to see her. And sooner than you expect, we would be on our way."

The gatekeeper shivered violently. He sat down on a nearby stool. Goose pimples sprouted all over his muscular body. How had the blind man known he was pulling up his *shirtsleeves?* Surely, he was blind. Or was it possible the cripple could see in one eye? One could never tell with some of these blind men. You could hardly cheat them in a game of cards. The gatekeeper would have loved to take a closer look at the blind man's eyes, to determine for himself if he was truly blind, or simply playing at being blind. But his guts failed him. With sweat pouring down his armpits, he scurried out, like a rat.

****

Six months ago, Effuah had visited the blind cripple. Clandestinely.

"I want you to make me a beauty queen," she cried breathlessly before she even had time to sit down on the dusty earth. "With the money I will win, I will build you a new house, take you to the biggest hospital there is and get your crippled legs and blind eyes fixed. I will give you enough money to buy the choicest piece of arable land. Your groundnut and millet farms will spread from here to the ends of the earth. You will own the fattest cows and goats, sheep and donkeys, chickens and ducks and guinea fowls. Sir, just make me a beauty queen and then, wish for anything. It will be all yours."

This had happened towards evening. The fierce April sun, though making its initial arrangement of quitting for the day was still burning. Effuah was drained. She sweated profusely from the desert heat, radiating from the scorched soil. Only moments before, a donkey cart had deposited her at the home of the crippled, blind man. She had journeyed over three hundred kilometres to meet him. It wasn't difficult locating him. Once she had arrived in the village of Vellingara where he lived, all she had to do was to mention his name. And as they say, the rest was history.

All Effuah ever wanted in life was to become a top model. She wanted to be like one of those 'gals' who posed on the covers of glossy magazines, which littered the shelves of the supermarkets in the city, advertising flashy cars, designers perfumes, skimpy lingerie and so on. When she wasn't thumping through glossy magazines on supermarket shelves, Effuah was browsing the Internet. She knew all the websites where she would find and download A3 sized pictures of her favourite models. She gawked at these printouts until every feature on her models' bodies was imprinted on her memory. It was all thanks to her high school for installing a computer lab and teaching them how to be computer literate. She browsed day in day out, even missing maths and science, boring subjects. Deep in her heart, she knew winning a beauty contest was the first step towards achieving her heart's desire of becoming a top model.

Effuah was indeed fit to be a beauty queen. And a model. She was tall, like her mentors on the covers of glossy magazines. She had a pointed nose, something African women who didn't have it would offer a limb for. She had a rich mass of hair, the envy of her friends. Effuah was beautiful.

On her own she had learned the proper manner of cat walking, a vital tool if you wanted to become a model. Every night before she went to bed, she practiced cat walking before the full-length mirror in her room. She could never catwalk enough. She was sure she would win if she joined any beauty contest. One was coming up soon. She had filled and submitted the application for it.

However, Effuah lacked the most important criteria necessary to become a winner. She had lost it right from birth. The culture, tradition and values of the society into which she was conceived and born ensured it was taken away from her. From the moment she took her first breath, and was stung by the dry, dusty air of her fatherland, her confidence had gone up in smoke. She was schooled and thought that survival had nothing to do with willpower; neither perseverance nor hard work. Soothsayers and witchdoctors were the answers. Whether you lived or died; whether you did well in life or not depended on them.

In her years of existence, Effuah had found that perhaps this was true. When she was ill, she did not go to the hospital for treatment. The witchdoctor who lived in the outskirt of town told her what and what to do. A boiled egg placed in the middle of a cross road; or a shot of oil and a handful of salt sprinkled at a junction was enough. She recovered as soon as she offered these sacrifices. She had amulets tied firmly on her waist to ward off evil spirits. She even had one particular amulet that prevented unwanted pregnancy. "Never go around without it," her mother had told her the day it was handed over to her. Effuah was thirteen years old then. Even though she didn't study hard enough, she had never failed any examination. A drink of the concoction made from chalk ensured that she chose the right options in objective tests and solved maths the right way, arriving at the appropriate answers of course.

****

After exhausting all manner of promises to the crippled, old man, Effuah gaped with large, watery eyes, which glowed in anticipation of some miracle. She listened, sucking in every single word the cripple uttered, not letting a morsel drop. The man was sprawled on a weather-beaten mat on the veranda of his dusty bungalow. As he spoke, he slapped away dozens of desert flies, which found his withered, sunburnt face and occluded eyes irresistible landing grounds. And he counted his prayer beads. He spoke in measured tones, breaking his sentences with the noisy gritting of what was left of his teeth; all stained a deep yellowish red by kola nut. With child-like sincerity, Effuah answered the simple, but deliberate questions he put to her.

"You want to become a beauty queen, eh?"

"By all means, sir."

"Becoming a beauty queen is not easy, you know."

"I vow to do everything necessary."

The cripple thought about this, drove away his flies, counted his beads. Effuah's heart pounded with anticipation. She wanted to cover his face with her scarf, and stop the flies from bothering him.

"You are ready to do anything, you say," the cripple said in his measured tone.

"Anything."

"You have to promise you will do whatever I ask when indeed you become a beauty queen."

Effuah was beside her self with joy.

"I promise. With all my heart. Just make me a beauty queen and I will be your slave."

"Two days before the contest, come back to me. It is what you want desperately, to become a beauty queen-"

"Yes, it is what I want desperately."

"Your wish will be granted."

Effuah was overwhelmed.

"May the almighty preserve you," she choked.

She hugged the blind, old cripple with all her strength, her bosom tightly pressed against his frail rib cage, her fingers dipping into the thin of his back. Hours after she had departed, the old cripple continued to gently rub the region of his chest where the young girl's breasts had rested. He sucked his parched, torn lips, tasting blood as he savoured the odd, but pleasurable sensation in his tired groin; a sensation which he had since learnt to forget.

****

From somewhere in the rear, the applause began. First one person stood up. Then another. Then another. Each clapped as loud as he could. Soon, like a communicable disease, everyone was afflicted. Finally, with all standing, the applause rose to an exhilarating crescendo. It sustained for what seemed forever. Effuah thought the roof of the auditorium would come crashing down on all heads. Hot tears came rushing down her flushed cheeks, washing away her delicately applied makeup. Adama, her best friend, and confidant, source of the old, blind, crippled man's address fawned over her. She dabbed Effuah's face with a scented white handkerchief, which the crippled old man had provided. It was on shaky legs that Effuah climbed the stage to be crowned. As the glittering, emerald and ruby studded crown rested on her head, Effuah heaved a long sigh of relief, which for the deafening applause would have reverberated all over the hall.

Effuah had beaten thirty-five other contestants to clinch the coveted crown. She was astonishing in her elegance, having found a willing sponsor in a well-known business tycoon. Mr. Business tycoon was quick to identify her potentials. He had agreed to bankroll her pursuit in return for a 'little something'. Effuah gave this 'little something', willingly. No price was too much to pay in her desire to become a top model.

Instantly, she was the centre of attraction. Local and international television crews converged on her, like carrion eaters on an exposed carcass.

"Tell us about yourself, more than we already know from your file."

"How happy are you?"

"Did you expect to win?"

"Do you have the full support of your parents, seeing that you are quite young, only seventeen…"

"What're your future ambitions?"

Future ambitions, Effuah thought. Only if they knew.

"Smile for the cameras."

Effuah beamed.

The cameras went off, *flash, flash, flash.* Blood rushed to her head. Highly placed, pot-bellied, bald-headed, mean-spirited government officials, chief executives and diplomats had their own hidden agenda. While congratulating her, they enquired *discretely.*

"Would the new queen be kind enough to attend a private dinner?" They would send their drivers to fetch her. She should name her car of choice. Venue? Her wish is their command. They would trade their right hands to share of the spoils. Effuah's answers were evident in her innocent, sweet smiles: Yes, it would be her pleasure.

Admirers sought her autograph, bringing books and cards and pictures to be autographed. Radio stations recorded her voice. Advertising agents fought over themselves, flirting with her there and then, wooing her like a new lover. Later at a press conference, more questions. More camera lights: red, green, yellow. Her perfect set of teeth kept glittering as the camera lights reflected off them. Drunk with attention, Effuah thought gaily, *I am made. Now, I will become a star.*

And overnight she became a celebrity. She was uprooted from her modest home in the squalid part of town to a plush office in the heart of town. She had managers. She had assistants. She had an assortment of clothes. Perfumes. Jewelleries. She had the latest makeup kits. All free from fashion and designer houses strewn across the country, and even beyond. She was chauffeur driven in a brilliant white BMW, the star prize for the winner of the beauty contest. Modelling and advertising contracts piled in, like manna from heaven. Happy was not a strong enough word to express Effuah's state of mind.

****

The gatekeeper trembled, even as he relayed his message. "Who is this person?" Mr. Bright, Effuah's Public Relations Officer asked, furious at the interruption. It was exactly three minutes before the cameras started rolling. They didn't have all day. There was that other auditioning for a cellular phone company's voice prompt. The company's secretary has been on his neck all morning.

"I don't know," the gatekeeper replied.

"Go. Ask him to come back some other time."

"Go and ask him yourself."

What insolence, everyone thought. What could have made the gatekeeper step out of his station, and answer so rudely? Effuah was particularly affronted. She had schemed and schemed and schemed, warming no fewer than three beds before she landed this contract of modelling, *Ecstasy.* She wanted to get the whole thing over and done with as quickly as possible.

"I will see him if he so adamant," she announced. "But I hope by God he doesn't want an autograph for his damned son, or daughter, because then, he wouldn't get one."

The gatekeeper rubbed his ample left earlobe vigorously. His armpits itched. If there was anything the old, crippled, blind, or semi blind man wanted, he was confident it wasn't an autograph for anybody. But he kept his conviction to himself.

On Effuah's heels were her entourage: managers, assistants, bodyguards, make-up specialists, the whole works. The gatekeeper brought up the rear. Solemnly. The sight of a wiry, old woman standing in the middle of the visitors' room filled Effuah with anger. She thought, Did Sany not say it was a man. Who the hell is this old hag? Then she glimpsed the crumpled bundle. Recognition hit her. She froze on her track. Not anticipating her sudden halt, her stooges rammed into her, nearly knocking her over. Her stomach walls knotted dangerously. She bent double. Recovering quickly, her entourage saw the reason for her discomfort. They watched Effuah and waited. Effuah let her raised shoulders slump. The presence of the formidable witchdoctor in the city, simply to seek her out spelt trouble. She felt faint. Reaching out frantically, she gripped an assistant's leg.

Sensing that Effuah was in the room, for the swift approaching footsteps he had heard moments ago had all come to a sudden halt, and sweet smelling perfumes now filled his nostrils, the old, crippled, man called out softly, "Young lady, are you there?"

Heavy silence accosted him. But he was not perturbed. He went on, "You remember me, I am sure, don't you?"

Patiently, he waited for an answer. When none was forthcoming, he carried on, still unperturbed, "I have waited these several months for you to come. But I didn't see you. I decided to come instead."

He paused here for Effuah. Then carried on, "You vowed you would do whatever I asked if I helped you become a beauty queen? That you would build me a new house, take me to the biggest hospital there was, and get my legs and eyes fixed. That you would give me enough money to buy the choicest piece of arable land, my groundnut farms would spread from here to the ends of the earth. You made so many other promises, remember?"

Effuah was amazed at the old man's acute memory. It was over six months now. And he still remembered! Confirming that she was there, and listening to him because of the tension he could feel in the electrified atmosphere, the old blind man continued softly, "I kept my part of the bargain. Now that you have achieved your heart's desire, you will be a good girl, won't you?"

Several seconds passed as he waited for an answer, getting none. But he knew she was there, listening to him, watching him, her breath suspended in tragic anticipation. Behind her, her entourage and others appeared dazed and spellbound, as if they had been jinxed. As the seconds dragged into minutes, muscles moved, eyes blinked, breaths were released, and Adam's apples rose and fell as people swallowed hard.

"Who is this mad blind man?" someone croaked.

Nobody had any kind of answer.

"What the heck does he want?" another whispered.

The old, crippled, blind man had his answer ready for them. However, he allowed them to stew and cook. After what seemed like an eternity, when he felt he could hear brain cells creak against each other, when he could feel muscles twitch and hearts flutter, he let out slowly, "Effuah Dado, you will be my number six wife."

Disorder reigned as shrill whistles rent the quietness of the visitors' waiting room. Effuah broke down. She sobbed uncontrollably. The old, blind cripple could hear her now, amidst the confusion. He imagined how beautiful she would be, how wonderful it would be to take her. An intense fire started in his lower regions. He knew that the young woman was powerless to resist him. She was a generous gift of the gods. After all, hadn't he been minding his own business when she quietly crept up and delivered herself to him?

As if on cue, everything became suddenly still seconds after the initial uproar. Continuing in his soft tone, the old, blind, cripple ended gravely, "I have come to take you home to Vellingara."

so, this is Lagos!

I had just completed my Joint Admissions and Matriculation Board (JAMB) Exams in June. After only two weeks of lazing away at home, idleness gnawed at my mind with mangled fingers, not unlike a terminal disease.

"If you're serious about keeping busy," my Auntie Felicia told me one Sunday, "come to the garage. I could use an extra hand in my restaurant."

I jumped and danced with glee. Here was an opportunity to explore Lagos, something my parents had never permitted me to do before.

Reason?

This is Lagos!

** **

I woke up by 4.30 a.m. the next day to travel from Festac town to Apapa where my auntie had her restaurant. Under normal circumstances, this was a distance that could be covered in 30 minutes. Even less. But then, in the dictionary of *our* Lagos, the term 'normal circumstances' did not have a place!

"Mama put," my twin brothers jeered at me as I briskly made my way out of the house. It was their custom to incense me at the slightest opportunity.

"Darling sweetie, have a nice day," my mother called out quickly from her bedroom. "And remember, this is Lagos."

I swallowed hard and said nothing.

"Darling sweetie," my mother placated, "did you hear me? I said, remember this is Lagos."

"I heard you mum," I replied sullenly, the words nearly gagging me. I was swollen with anger, and needed only just a little, *'fuuuurrrrrrrrrr',* to float away; or a tiny, tiny prick to go, *'buuurrrrsssstttt'.* My mother knew the signs, and was intent on stopping the quarrel, which she knew would ensue. She had heard my brothers' annoying remark of, 'Mama put.' However, her bribe of 'Darling Sweetie', did not stop me from fluttering my bushy eyebrows at my brothers, cutting them into bits and pieces with my large, brown eyes, and lashing back with a shrill, angry cry of:

"Maltex bottles!"

And for this, all I got was *'Monkey teeth',* as teeth and gums, akin to a braying donkey's, were bared at me, followed by peals of mocking laughter as they disappeared in the general direction of the bathroom. The need to get ready for school temporarily overshadowed any bitterness they felt for my comparing them with the short bottles of the malted drink, Maltex. That they would hit back at me for reminding them that they were *'shorties'* was a forgone conclusion.

But I was ready for them.

Let them just try!

****

It was a dark morning. Cold wind loaded my nostrils with smells of putrefying garbage. In the distance, stray, straggly dogs struggled to outdo each other as they barked wickedly. Chaperoned by termites in nuptial flight, dull yellow streetlights, which failed to discriminate between puddles and potholes only added to my frustration. I waddled, slipped and caught myself just in time; lurched about like a drunkard and struck my toes on mean, but innocent looking objects. As I stumped along to the bus stop, I fumed:

It wasn't as if I was going to be a 'Mama put.' After all, did Auntie Felicia not have a real restaurant?

'Mama puts' represented those women food vendors, who sold their stuffs at street corners. Images of poor and less privileged Lagosians handing over plates to the women, crying, *'Mama put fifty Naira beans'* or *'Mama put twenty five Naira garri'* in the fashion of beggars soliciting for alms came flooding my mind's eye. Those brothers of mine! Thinking of them left a sour taste in my mouth.

One day...just one day soon.

****

"So you could make it," Auntie Felicia cried in a loud, loud voice. "I'd since given up on you."

"I lost my way at first and had to ask people for directions to *Felic Super Restaurant.*"

"Well, you're here now, it's only past eight. I'll have to take Bisi to the market with me. We've run short of almost everything...

Bisi!

Bisi!

Are you not ready yet, Bisi?"

The way my Aunty Felicia was shouting, one would have thought that Bisi was in Kafanchan, thousands of kilometers away. Or stone deaf. She was like that, my Auntie Felicia. Very boisterous. Right now, she was counting her money, packing her pieces of black and blue and white polyethylene bags together, collecting her empty cans and plastics of palm and groundnut oil and doling instructions out to Bisi, all at once.

"Bisi, check if the curry is still remaining, check, quickly, quickly, where is the container."

"No, madam it is almost finished."

"Ahhhh Bisi! Bisi! Finished or almost finished? Finished or almost-?"

"Okay, I will say finished," Bisi replied, casting a quick glance in my direction. I took a look at the curry container.

Hmmmm....

"Bring let me see for myself. Olorun Jesu!" my Auntie Felicia exploded. "My Gad...d-d-do you call this finish?"

"Well, madam, since I don't know when next we would be going to the market, I thought-"

"You thought what? This is how you serve my food away to customers eh? This is how you serve my food away to customers eh, and month after month, year after year I struggle and struggle and struggle without seeing neither head nor tail of what I am -"

"Sorry madam."

"It is yourself you should be sorry for. One day you will open your own restaurant. I will see whether you will not fold up and return to Ifetedo in a matter of days. This is Lagos! How many times will I tell you, this is Lagos, you must learn to be sharp. Open your eyes, open your eyes for heaven's sake. This is Lagos! This is Lagos!"

We were probably the same age, Bisi and I. But she looked dull. Maybe it was because she was not educated, else how could she have taken one-quarter full to mean finished? Didn't she know that this was Lagos, that one needed to be shrewd?

"Ibironke, can you manage without us."

All thoughts of Bisi and her foolishness vanished from my mind.

"Yes, auntie, I can try-"

"It is either you can manage or you can't. Which one do you mean?"

"I can manage-"

"Bisi, show her how to dish."

I opened my eyes as Bisi demonstrated to me how to dish.

"Bisi let's go or are you planning to take a whole week explaining just how to measure out fifty Naira rice and fifty Naira pepper soup to Ibironke? ...Ibironke my dear, take care and I hope you have a good selling hand."

"My hand is very good auntie."

Next thing I saw, Auntie Felicia and Bisi were tearing away at top speed, their feet hardly touching the ground. Then they jumped into a speeding and overcrowded *molue* and the van sped on, with the conductor beckoning passengers at the top of his hoarse voice. Two other commuters- an elderly man and a woman with a baby on her back- tried imitating my Auntie and Bisi. But they ended up ramming into each other, landing squarely on the tarmac. Horns blared angrily, but the vehicles only swerved and did not stop. A traffic policeman, two paces away pretended he did not hear the child howling painfully on its mothers back and simply walked on.

I exhaled slowly.

****

After about two hours, no customer had lifted the curtains of *Felic Super Restaurant* to come asking for food of any kind, not even drinks. How was I to justify my 'Good Selling' hand to my Auntie Felicia? Rubbing my palms together as if in solemn supplication, I went outside to take a look around.

The day had come fully awake, and the garage was a study in noises. Everywhere, horns hooted and blared; people shouted and cursed; conductors engaged each other in fist fights as they struggled for passengers; hawkers hollered attention to their wares; babies wailed from their mother's backs; traffic policemen threatened unrepentant drivers; and shopkeepers watched out for thieves who were ready to steal anything ...even packs of faeces, if well presented!

Trailers and lorries billowed thick, black smoke into the atmosphere, and the bluish-black air tasted funny, like burnt rubber. A frail, old man covered in fine sprays of something white suddenly sauntered from nowhere and sat on the bonnet of a seemingly abandoned taxi. From within the taxi, somebody instantly got up. Hurriedly, this somebody shoved a baldhead out of the front passenger's window, and made to grab at the old man. The distance thwarted him.

"People! People, see me see trouble O," he roared thunderously, with eyes blazing like red-hot coals. "Daddy! ...yu wan' condemn my shock absorbers? Eh? ...Yu wan' put sand-sand for my *garri*? ...If dem sen' you, I beg, tell dem say you no see me, you hear?"

The old man glimpsed the terror in the red eyes, and the hatred in the voice. His astonished face seemed to protest:

I am not responsible for your frustrations, boy. So don't hang it on me!

And like an alley cat caught stealing fish, he scampered off. Selecting another object, this time an abandoned petty trader's wooden table, he sat down. When he was sure no body was going to molest him again, he set about his business. Bending down with hands on his knees, and mouth wide open, he coughed and coughed and coughed until his eyes, blood red now, smarted and watered. Finally done with his rib-racking cough, he blew his nostrils vigorously, rubbing the mucus with the back of his right and left hands. He then inspected his handiwork for several long seconds, and swiftly proceeded to wipe the back of his hands on his trousers, his consternated demeanor clearly screaming:

This thick, stinking, green and yellow mucus can't have come from my body. No!

I am not sick, that I know!

Hungry, yes, but not sick!

After resting a while to catch his breath, the old man, like a soldier, continued matching on stoically as if he had never stopped. If anyone cared to investigate, this frail, old man was going nowhere.

****

The two men were superbly dressed. The strong scent of their expensive perfumes pervaded the restaurant, obliterating the aromas of fish, meat, rice, beans, *eba, amala* and other cooked food. After taking their seats and carefully setting down their expensive suitcases, they turned their attention to me.

"Lady, serve us the best you have to offer," the taller of the two addressed me quietly in the manner of a gentleman. He wore an ox-blood colored guinea brocade, with an elaborate design of land tortoise on it.

Very expensive!

And I prepared to listen as I dished and served them.

"You're looking so well, Reginald."

"And you too, Livinus."

"Oh boy, I have missed you."

"And me too, I have missed you."

They were old friends who had not set eyes on each other since graduation, seven years ago. Livinus was a Lagos-based business consultant, while Reginald was visiting from Ibadan where he represented one of the major banks. He was dressed in the typical banker's fashion: a well-tailored navy blue suit, with matching trousers and shoes. Gold cufflinks with which he buttoned the white long-sleeved shirt inside his suit caught my eyes:

Yves St. Laurent!

I envied them their success.

"Don't you have something to cool down with?" Reginald, with his mouth loaded with goat meat suddenly asked, catching me pants down in my eavesdropping act.

I indicated the cold bottle of water on the table before them. The two friends ached their eyebrows:

"Ha, ha, ha," they laughed out, loud and clear.

"Hey lady, we need something to get us started for the day," Reginald said, still laughing.

"Don't you sell beer?" Livinus clarified.

"No, no sir, but I am sure I could get some from across the street."

"And don't you have anyone to assist you in here?" Reginald asked, this time, kindly.

"My Auntie has gone to the market with the other help. They won't be back for a while."

Both friends looked at each other. Reginald face registered pity for me. I was touched by his kindness.

"What are you waiting for then?" Livinus asked, not unkindly.

"And while you are at it, please serve us another plate of stew containing just fish," Reginald demanded.

They could pay!

I *know! I know they can pay.*

I loaded two sizeable plates with the best portions of fish from the stew pot and placed it before them. Immediately they attacked it hungrily. I did my humble calculations and was impressed. My only fear was if Auntie Felicia would ever let me go once she discovered how good my 'Selling Hand' was.

****

It was to the shop opposite *Felic Super Restaurant.* The shopkeeper took one look at me and his face brightened.

"Hallo *titi,*" he crooned, exposing a bucal cavity devoid of any healthy tooth. Everything had been painted brown, or was it black by tobacco.

"Did you come to visit old Alphonso Aloysius Alao?"

I couldn't help smiling. This seemed to put him in a lighter frame of mind.

"Hmmm...I knew it as soon as I woke up this morning... that ... that something great was going to happen to me today... Tell me..."

If I left this Mr. Alphonso Aloysius Alao, he was going to croon all day like an infant. So I went straight to the point.

"Look sir, my auntie owns that restaurant opposite."

"Oh, so, you are the one. You are Ibironke, the one that will soon be going to the university..."

My auntie had already spread the word around.

"Well...yes," I smiled broadly. "You see, sir, there are these important guests at the restaurant now. They want some beers, and seeing that you are just opposite and sell drinks, and we don't, I was wondering-"

"Do not be wondering again, my fine *titi*, very beautiful gal. You see, it was a perfect arrangement between your auntie, Feli, and my humble self, Prince...Prince Alphonso Aloysius Alao. I will direct customers to her and when she needs drinks, she will come to me...So just tell me how many crates you want."

"I just want only four bottles of Star, sir."

"Forget that sir business, *titi* Just call me Prince ...Prince Aloy. Now did you say only four bottles ...is that not too small? These Lagos men can drink O, and when your auntie can, which is most of the time, she can make them drink up to three crates at a seating. I think you should obtain more."

"No sir... I mean Prince-"

"Prince Aloy."

"Yes, Prince Aloy-"

"That is it, Prince Alphonso Aloysius Alao-"

"Let me just begin with just four bottles. If they want more, I will come back, at least you are not closing now, are you?"

"Me?" he asked, thumping his chest furiously with one thick finger, as if the very idea of closing then was a sacrilege. "Close now? ...For where? What on earth for?"

"Then no problems."

"You are very very right."

Mr. Alphonso was grinning from ear to ear now. I shirked from him when he came a little too close.

"Is like you are a very intelligent girl, eh?" he flattered. "Frankly speaking I like intelligent girls. In fact, I will give any thing ...any amount of *money* in this world just to be close to them, I swear."

Funny old man! Why is he winking at me?

"Sir, can I have the drinks now please, my customers are waiting."

"Not sir, *titi* I say call me Aloy, and why not? You can have the drinks any time."

While handing over a polyethylene bag containing four bottles of very chilled beer, he made to rub my arm, smiling crookedly. I cast him a killer glance as I snatched the polyethylene bag and fled, as if pursued by the devil.

"What of the money, fine *titi*," he cried.

"As soon as they pay me, I will come over and balance you. I am not going to disappear, am I?" I called back.

"Oh that's no problem. That's how your auntie Feli and I used to do it. But even if you didn't pay me, I will collect it somehow somehow," he shouted after me, cackling.

"I-will-pay-you-your-dammed-money," I replied, spitting the words at him.

****

They drank, discussed big money, big business and talked about sweet, good, old days long gone by. What wonderful appetite! Four more times I rushed to Prince Aloy for more beers. And four more times I visited the stew and soup pots...for more fish and goat meat, liver, kidney, *shaki* and even *kpomo*...The pots were nearly empty of everything now!

And I watched them like cinema as they ate and drank, for they made an interesting duo. Suddenly gazing at his wristwatch, which glittered despite the limited light straining into the restaurant, Livinus exclaimed:

"Can you imagine, Regi? We have been here for close to two hours without knowing it."

"Our bill lady," Reginald called quickly, after confirming the time by a quick glance at his equally glittering Rolex. They were suddenly in a hurry to get back to their lucrative businesses. As I handed the bill over, both friends rose from their seats, struggling for it, one pinning the other down.

"Don't do that Livi", Reginald said, laughing. "Let me pay."

"No, I will pay," Livinus cried, out of breath. Unlike his friend, he wore a serious grin.

"Next time, you can settle, Livi, but today, please give me the privilege."

"No Regi. You pay next time. Today, I will pay, pronto," Livinus insisted.

Soon the argument got heated up.

I sighed painfully.

"I said I would pay for God's sake!" Reginald shouted.

"No Regi, you wont for heaven's sake," Livinus shouted back. "I will pay, I, Livinus Adewale, will pay, I will damn pay!"

Poor friends, I thought. How can they be fighting over who was going to settle an ordinary bill? I prayed for divine wisdom as I watched them about to go for each other's throats, snarling like wild dogs, facial muscles tensed, sweat budding and beginning to slide down their faces and drip onto the table.

Soon, their voices rose higher:

"I must pay this bill and no one else."

"That is a blatant lie!"

How embarrassing!

"Gentlemen ...please, please," I cried. An idea had suddenly struck me, and I stopped short of screaming at them. "Take it easy. Maybe I can help you."

They suspended their argument and stood aback, each breathing hard, like people who had ascended mountain Kilimanjaro in record time. They then surveyed me as, if like a UFO, I had just zoomed out of mars and landed here on earth.

"How might you help us, young lady," Reginald asked while Livinus, with eyes flashing, glared at me with mistrust.

"Here," I said, smiling as I loosened the silk head tie around my waist. The two friends gawked at my fully developed pelvic, catching their breaths. In a moment, their eyes strained upwards and rested squarely on my heaving chest. But I didn't care. What was more important to me was how to settle the small problem of who was going to foot their bill. I didn't wish their friendship to come to an abrupt end, and knew beyond reasonable doubts that that would be the case if no settlement were reached soon.

"Take it," I commanded, handing the head tie over to Livinus who accepted it with trepidation, as if it would suddenly spring and deal him a lethal bite.

"And what might I do with it, my dear lady?" he queried cautiously.

"Here is what you will do."

****

It was Reginald who blindfolded me with the head tie. The idea I had cleverly devised was that while blindfolded, I would attempt to touch one of them. Whoever was lucky enough for me to touch him would then pay the bill! At first, they didn't want to accept it, but then I succeeded in convincing them that my idea was entirely democratic, with no chance whatsoever for cheating.

The blindfold was a little bit too tight. But I didn't mind. Why, no pain was too much to bear in preserving the brotherhood between two progressive young men. Besides, the exercise was going to last for only a few seconds.

Excited now, I began groping for both men. Moving towards the place where I knew they stood moments ago, I groped and encountered empty space, and my heart missed one beat. Moving haphazardly in all directions, and simultaneously doing a complete 360 degrees, with my arms fully outstretched, I encountered again, nothing but emptiness. This time my heart missed two to three beats, and inwardly, I cried:

Haaaaa!

And just as sudden, the restaurant seemed a little too quiet for my liking. I broke out in cold sweat, and with my heartbeats now in disarray, my heart began hammering against my ribs.

What was I doing blindfolded before two complete strangers. Suppose they took advantage of me, blindfolded as I was?

Suddenly, it felt as if a mighty hand, like a demonic vice, was clutching my throat, threatening to choke the living daylight out of me. I tore ferociously at my blindfold, which had now assumed the status of a live adversary, with blood pumping through its veins. God, was the *thing* tight? With all the strength I could muster, I fought the blindfold. For what seemed like an eternity, we wrestled, the blindfold and I. As if in delirium, I kept whimpering as I fought for my life!

Help me, God!

Goddddddddddd!

God please come and hellllllllp me!!!

At last, I succeeded in tearing it away. While vigorously rubbing my eyes to restore the free flow of blood, I saw shadows of the two men around me, and my heart knew boundless joy, leaping to the high heavens.

Thank you God!

But then, by the time my eyes got accustomed to the dim light in the restaurant, these shadows, like a mirage on a searing hot day had melted and dissolved into absolute nothingness. Deep fear, starting from my back, crept steadily up my neck, like a coarse giant hand.

No!

No, no, no!!

Quickly and on all fours, I crept under the tables with alacrity, searching frantically for *my* men. Standing up without thinking, I bumped my head hard against the roof of the long table. Stars, brilliantly colored, and in their millions super-saturated my being.

Jesus Christ!

Raw pain stung me...like *koboko** to my bare skin. Dazed and out of breath, I scrambled out from under the table, tearing at my freshly re-touched hair with all ten fingers, dislodging three of my mother's artificial nails, which she had lent me in the process. Again on all fours, and creeping like a fugitive, I searched behind the doors, and like a mad woman, I rushed outside to check.

Nothing! Nothing!

Haaaaaa!

I stole a quick glance at Prince Alphonso Aloysius Alao. He was waving madly with both hands, trying to catch my attention.

Hell!

Helllllll!

Last time I was in his shop, out of rage, I nearly slapped his face for him, but for the strands of white hairs sprinkled all over his ugly, vulture-like scalp. Imagine grabbing me playfully on my buttocks and squeezing lasciviously! What did he take a small girl like me, only seventeen years old for? *Ashewo*...a prostitute?

Angry and confused, I tore back inside and going down on all fours again, searched behind the counter where the pots of rice and stew and pottage were. I tried behind the doors, and under the tables...yet again.

Nothing!

Haaaaaa!

My blouse, a body hug, which I had worn to announce my flat stomach, was suddenly too tight. I was going to rend it when I remembered where I was:

In a motor garage in the very centre of Lagos!

Collapsing heavily on the floor like a bag of meal, I grabbed my head in agony. Streams of hot tears stung my eyes, blinding me. They then cascaded down my cheeks. I let them flow uninterrupted into my open mouth and wished the ground would open and swallow me. When the ground would not, I shuddered violently as several thoughts ran riot in my brain:

How on earth will I pay that cradle snatcher, that paedophile, Prince Aloy for all his beers? What will my brothers say when this news hit the headlines? They will taunt me to the very ends of this wicked earth! Ahhhh! Auntie Felicia... she would call me a fool, a nonentity. She would argue that the money spent in sending me through secondary school was wasted, thrown to the dogs, a perfect case of washing one's hands to crack palm kernels for chickens! And Bisi! Was I not literary laughing at her

---

* horsewhip

113

when she took one-quarter full for empty?
Ahhhhhhhhhhh!!!
Fear, and shame clutched my heart with cruel, cold hands.
So this is Lagos!
So this is Lagos!!
Flinging my hands into the air, I screamed as bile, bitter as brown ale, from deep within my guts, rose to my mouth:
Aaaaaaaaaahhhhhhhhhhhhhhhh dear God…. dear God…..
SO THIS IS LAGOS! SO THIS IS LAGOS!!

the street hawker and the herdsman

The girl ate the man up and down with her eyes as he hurriedly undressed. Catching her staring at him, he said, "Fine girl, don't worry. It is nothing. In fact you will enjoy it." Then he slinked closer as he stepped out of the last of his clothing. He smelt. The body odour wafted to her. It was the smell of weeks old sweat, stale, rancid, musky. She wrinkled her nostrils. Then she realised he had worn no briefs. Her jaws dropped. She never thought any sane person, man or woman, would walk about without briefs. Her shock of discovering that he was 'briefless' had hardly subsided when a small, strangled scream choked her.

"Oh, this thing will kill me," she cried.

"It will not kill you," the man said. His beady eyes shifted left and right, like a caged rat's. His member, now rigid was curved downwards from the cap. It pulsated at intervals, nodding. A fully-grown woman would have found it formidable. And the girl was barely fifteen.

"It will kill me. You see how it is long?" she said, adamant.

"What kind of human being are you, even?" the man said. He was furious. But he calmed down. Anger and impatience would get him no nearer his target. He knew he was dealing with an, 'undeflowered' girl. He thought they no longer existed. He changed his tactics.

"You are ripe now," he said, flashing his black and scattered dentition. "See this thing, how it is pointing. It can blind someone."

He was intent on boosting the girl's confidence. Success depended on it. The girl did not understand. She sought clarification.

"What can blind someone?" she said.

"This your breast," he said. "See how it is pointing. Like needle."

The man had by now successfully undone the zip on the girl's green threadbare blouse, slipping it halfway down her slim hands, her snaking veins bulged and standing firm. The girl, terribly baffled was still pondering the idea of how breasts could blind. Pointing shyly and straining to look downwards at her now fully exposed robust breasts, she argued vehemently:

"Breasts can't blind."

The man was suddenly irritated. He let the girl's blouse, which had completely come off her hands drop to the floor. He took in her young hips, just beginning to shoot out. He noted the soft, silky pubic hairs straining out of thin fabric of faded panties, scarcely able to contain her ample buttocks. He noted her flat, muscular stomach; noted the tiny belly button, like a black pea. He gulped air, his Adam's apple bobbing wildly, his member aching, nodding, radiating heat. This whole tête-à-tête was getting uncomfortably protracted, the man thought. And complicated too. He must end it once and for all and get on with the business he had in mind. He snarled angrily.

"You want the money or not?"

****

They were inside a dilapidated, out-of-the-way classroom. The man's bare necessities were strewn about in a corner, behind a cluster of broken chairs and lockers. It was here, behind this cluster of broken chairs and lockers that the man slept. It was here that he had successfully goaded the girl. And had gone ahead to make his proposal, a suggestions that the girl never dreamed of. The girl was shocked, and said so in as many words:

"May God forbid bad thing!"

"You mean to tell me you have never 'do' before," the man challenged.

"Do what?"

"Don't worry then," the man said conciliatorily. "I will buy everything in your tray. No need for a fine girl like you to be suffering in this hot sun."

The man watched hopefully as the girl considered his proposal. He was right about the issue of the hot sun, the girl thought. These days, the sun was unusually hot. Everything seemed to be ablaze. And recently too, the girl thought, her mother had scolded her severely for bringing back her wares unsold, only for most of them to get rotten and be thrown away. The losses incurred.. Her mother already owed a lot to those from whom she bought her goods. How happy her mother would be if for once she came back home with her wares all sold.

On full-foliaged mango trees outside, ravens cooed plaintively; out in the field, the man's cows, which he had left to herd themselves mooed, seeking attention. The man was a conscientious herdsman. He never joked with his flock. In fact, he lived for them. But for now, he failed to hear their call. Instead, he was proceeding to help the girl make up her mind. He licked his dried lips.

"Your mother will be happy with you if you sell everything in your tray. If you bring nothing back, but money."

The girl swallowed hard. She recalled yesterday. She had come back with one-quarter of her wares unsold. It was the ideal opportunity for her mother to give her a dressing down. Her mother didn't let the chance pass: My daughter, you are very lazy. Why do you keep bringing back your wares, eh? Where do you think I will get money to feed you and your brothers and sister? Look at your mates. Titi for instance. She doesn't bring anything back, not even a finger of banana. Why don't you do like Titi?

It was by chance one afternoon that the girl had discovered how Titi sold all her wares. She confronted Titi. Titi defended herself.

"If I don't bring this money, they will starve."

By 'they', Titi was referring to her junior brothers and sisters-all seven of them.

"I have to do it," Titi went on. "Since my ma fell ill, there is nobody to help. My dada doesn't care. Besides, it does not always hurt, except when he is rough. Like today. He gives me extra money too. I can buy earrings and new panties. See?"

Raising her gown, Titi showed the girl her new underwear, gift from her man-friend. The fabric was cool, and soft to the touch. The girl liked the purple lace by the hems.

****

The girl was shocked. The jovial herdsman had changed. She hugged herself, noticing her nakedness for the first time. What was she to do? As she thought about his proposal, knowing how her mother would react if she brought back her wares unsold, her heart softened. She might as well do like her friend, Titi. Let the man have his way if it would make her mother stop berating her everyday.

The girl whimpered and moaned, caught her lips with her teeth, clutched a chair leg, clawed at the floor as the herdsman sawed his way, struggling to penetrate. There was a tear, then a searing pain. The girl let out a short wail; then gave out a sustained moan. She couldn't make up her mind who to blame. Her mother who wouldn't let her be; or Titi who told her it wouldn't hurt.

"Please stop," she cried. "It is paining me."

The more she pleaded, the more the man dug. Suddenly, she felt warm wetness about her. Pushing with all her strength, she glimpsed bright red

117

blood trickling down her inner thighs. Her fears of moments ago gave way to hysteria. She began to sob, at first faintly, then loudly. The herdsman, intent on his mission was oblivious of her discomfort. He was a mask, his eyes shut tightly; his face contorted. She took one look at him amid the hot tears blinding her and feared for her life. She began to scream. But the man deftly clasped a crooked hand over her mouth. What became of her screams were whimpers.

||*|*

The herdsman had been at the job of cornering the street hawker for the past several weeks. Each time it seemed as if he was going to succeed, something had cropped up and ruined his efforts. The last time, one of his cows had developed instant madness. It had began running wild. He loved his animals. And had to abandon his carefully planned scheme to go after it. The pride of any herdsman was the well being of his cattle. Love for a woman did not interfere in that relationship.

Once every year, the herdsman would make the compulsory trip down south with his herd of cattle in search of pasture, travelling over a thousand kilometres. This mid-western town was where he preferred to pitch his tent. Here, the rain fell steadily. The grasses in the compounds of the numerous grammar schools grew long and lush. Sometimes, he envied his cattle as they munched away, green fluids dripping down the sides of their mouths. This was his eleventh voyage. In all that time, he had never come across a more beautiful girl. Most importantly, there were no complications. He had learnt from the girl that her father was dead.

Yesterday afternoon, he had seen her for the umpteenth time as she hawked fruits and nuts in the neighbourhood of the vast grammar school. As usual, he jested with her.

"My wife..."

"Who is your wife?"

"You," the man said, flashing his scattered dentition, his idea of a romantic smile.

The girl smiled shyly, scouting the ground. She didn't want the man to get the impression that she was laughing at his rotten teeth.

"I will marry you."

The girl said nothing.

"If you will agree to marry me, I will dash you one man cow and one woman cow. Soon you will have a herd like mine."

The girl smiled. All the while, her white tray, laden with groundnut and cashew nut and green oranges and yellow bananas lay balanced on her head, shading her, like an umbrella from the fierce sun. To reduce the pressure of the load, and to prevent it from messing up her newly plaited hair, a piece of brown cloth was neatly folded in the manner of a coiled millipede and placed in the centre of her head.

The man said, "Don't you like cows?"

The girl surveyed the field. Scattered around were cows of various sizes and ages. A gentle wind began to blow, carrying the odor of the grazing animal towards them. Thought of day old sawn grasses came to her mind. The girl imagined how much one of those cows would fetch in the market. If she were to sell even one cow, it would solve all their financial problems. But she was sure he was only joking. He can't be serious about giving away one male and one female cattle just for the fun of it. Unlike other days when he just simply flirted, this time the man pushed harder.

"Come tomorrow, you hear?" the man said. "Come when people have go to church? I will buy plenty groundnut and banana from you."

"But I have groundnut and banana here. Why not buy now."

"I have no money today. Tomorrow, I will have lots of money. I want to sell one of my cows."

"Okay," the girl said and began to drift away.

The man eyed her young bosom and licked his charred lips, hating his terribly dry skin. He transferred his herdsman's stick, which he had been leaning on from his right hip to his neck, hooking it on either side with one hand. He may not be able to give the girl a cow. That was not possible. But if she cooperated, he would give her lots of money. He had enough to spare.

"I will let you keep the change even," the man shouted after the receding back.

As the girl went along, she imagined how much money she would make from selling her fruits to him tomorrow. And he said he would let her keep the change.

Sunday dawned bright. By ten o'clock the neighbourhood was deserted. The girl did not go to church. She told her mother she wished to start hawking earlier, so as to sell off everything on her tray. Her mother thought it was a good idea.

Just when he was giving up hope, the man sighted the girl approaching from the distance. Her tray, laden with fruits was perfectly balanced on her head. The girl wasted no time delving into her first bargain of the day.

"How much banana and groundnut you want?"

"I will buy plenty," the man said.

"Then buy," the girl said, her voice impatient. "Or have you not sold the cow yet?"

"I have, but the money is not here."

"So where is the money?"

"It is in my place," the man said, pointing.

The girl knew his place. It was one of those fallen classroom blocks in the distance, which she could see, even from here. She had often seen him retire there.

"Let us go there," the man said. "I will let you have the change."

The girl was excited again. She let him round up his cows and lead them towards his place. Then she followed behind.

****

The women heard the whimpers first. They nudged themselves questionably.

"Where is it coming from?" one of them whispered.

The group of several men and women, members of a local church had at the last moment decided to take the disused road which ran through the grammar school in a bid to catch up time, being already late for a fortnightly prayer meeting at their sister church on the other side of the school. Soon the men heard the whimpers too. The women began to hesitate out of curiosity.

"Sisters, how late can we be?" their leader pleaded. "Let's get on with our business."

But the women were no pushovers. Feminine instincts warned them of what might be going on. Cautiously, they traced the source of the unnerving sound.

"Isn't that the tray of one of these girls selling things?" one of them pointed out.

The girl's white tray, fully laden was absentmindedly placed in a windowpane. The men saw it. They knew at once what was going on. In a flash, they were bounding towards the classroom, the women right behind them, church meeting forgotten.

In order not to warn the perpetrator of their approach, they tiptoed through the last paces to the classroom. Some looked through broken windows; others through the door. The sight of a teenage girl sprawled on the floor, struggling weakly as a grown man pounded away on her, his hands firmly clasped against her mouth, was incomprehensibly appalling. Rooted to the ground, they stared, mouths open. As one woman went into a fainting spell, others threw up what they had had for breakfast.

Just as sudden, the herdsman realized he had company. He opened his eyes. Several pairs of angry, blazing eyes burnt into his. Everything stood still. For how long, no one would be able to tell later, but like magic, action resumed at a much heightened pace again somewhere along the line. Seeing that he had been caught red-handed he sprang off the girl, his erect manhood dripping blood and seminal fluid as it pulsated. "Bastards," he muttered angrily in his native tongue.

Reaching for his browned out caftan carelessly thrown aside, he grabbed and drew from it the needlepoint, glittering dagger, which he always carried. Sighting this, everyone of the church group took off, the women's voices ululating resoundingly as they fled.

****

The herdsman pondered his predicament for the thousandth time. Two things bothered him. He would presently take care of the first. But the second? It was more painful. He knew he was going to be punished severely. But the fact was that he did not even achieve orgasm. He was there, but not quite. He did not feel his body tremble; did not hear himself bellow. How bad can anything get, he wondered. It was because he was from other parts, from the north, that was why they would ensure he drew a heavy punishment. Were it in his parts, he would have gotten off with a light punishment, if he were punished at all. It wasn't as if the girl died. Only minor bruises, which she brought upon herself by wriggling and wriggling and wriggling. And maybe that little tear in the mouth; nothing a doctor who knew his worth couldn't handle. And of course, he was true to his words. He paid her. Generously. He put the notes inside her tray, wedging them with a bunch of banana. Had she seen that kind of money before?

His mind was made up. He would not allow the local authorities to have the last laugh. They may jail him, imprison him, kill him, but they would never have his beloved cattle. He would teach them not to expect to reap where they did not sow. Did they think he didn't know their scheme, that as soon as he was safely in prison and out of the way, they would move in quickly and auction his animals, growing fat on his sweat? Did they know how long he had been herding those animals? They were over forty cows now. He started with only two, his inheritance when his father died. The police were in for a giant-sized surprise when they arrived. He knew they were already on their way.

And the herdsman put his razor-sharp dagger to immediate use as he took care of the first of his bothers. He started with the males and worked fast. Each animal he went to, he gripped its testicles, sliced it neatly in one fell swoop, watched the testicle drop to the ground. He did not wait for the animal to crumble in a heap before moving to the next. One after another he seized a testicle, sliced with all his strength, yanked, warm blood spraying his arms and face and legs.

"Reap where you did not sow, will you," he shouted in his mother tongue as he worked. "Reap where you did not sow."

He kicked grass, fell and stood up, his hands and body all sand and blood. He sobbed as he went from one animal to the next, yanking off testicles, jumping away quickly. Soon the animals recognized they were in danger. They bounded away as he approached. He chased and chased and chased. Finally tired, he crumbled to the ground. He hid his face in his bloodied hand; allowed his dagger to slip to the ground beside him. He wept bitterly. How bad can anything possibly get, he wondered again and again and again.

10

The man and the girl

Earlier on in the evening, the girl had glimpsed him. He of the saxophone, he of the cleft lip; of the slight stutter. She had quickened her steps in another direction. But the man had seen her. She could feel the earth's slight tremor from his every step transmit to her from behind. His voice reached her ears.

"Where are you off to now, my beautiful maiden?"

The girl could not bring herself to stop. Or answer. She walked on, resolutely. The man trotted after her, his limp more pronounced than ever. The man wished he were younger. Perhaps, if he were, just perhaps...

"You will be at the grand dance tonight, won't you, my maiden?" the man said.

The girl slowed down.

"Yes," she said, her voice trembling.

"Surely you will dance for me, then?" the man, slowing down too, continued, panting and spraying her face with spittle. She did not answer, but turned her face away, preferring instead to stare at her feet. She didn't like the way his thin, rough skin, like parchment, visible through his torn singlet flailed in and out, as if it would suddenly snag on the jutting rib bones and tear and the man would collapse. What would she do then?

The girl still didn't understand why her heart always beat faster whenever she ran into this man. Maybe it was the fear. But how was it that this same fear dissolved like ice brought near a raging fire when he was playing his saxophone and she was dancing? In those instances, with the villagers yelling at the top of their voices at what she was doing with her feet and waist and chest, she even found herself drawn to him, like iron fillings to a magnet. It was ironic. It always seemed then as if her life depended on the sounds emanating from his rusting musical instrument. They were a pair in these circumstances, she and the man with the split upper lip.

The girl had long noted that the man did not apply himself to his saxophone when he played for the other girls. She could tell that the saxophone sounded differently when he played for her. And the man knew this too. Didn't his eyes come alive and shine as bright as the stars? Didn't he lose all semblance of composure, becoming carefree, like a babe in the presence of its mother? Didn't he follow her every movement- her feet, her hands, her buttocks, all rising and falling in unison as if by magic; as if in a dream?

The girl's confusion, which prevented her from replying to the man's question, 'Surely you will dance for me, then?' had been clearly evident from her countenance. Her shoulders slumped and sweat beads broke out on her face. She was embarrassed, knowing that she had lingered too long. Afraid that the man, whom she knew missed nothing, would misinterpret everything, she made to shuffle on. But the man chose to play on her confusion.

"I know where you are off to…to the riverside, to await your grandmother's return from her farm on the other side of the river," he stuttered, spraying her a generous amount of spittle. "But stay awhile with me, my beautiful maiden. Come. I will milk you some milk from my cows. It will do you good after tonight's dance."

"No, thank you," the girl said, a little too quickly.

"Perhaps next time then?"

This time a mischievous smile played on his dried, weather-beaten lips.

"I-I d-don't know," the girl said.

The man, now facing the girl took in her blouse; noted the small tear by the armpit; feasted his eyes on her bosom.

"Tomorrow?" the man said, his eyes glinting; his voice soft.

"I don't know," the girl said, her voice raised a little.

The girl moved away without raising her head. She was gone before the man had a chance to begin another round of small talk, or tried to make her follow him by promising something else. The man caressed his gray goatee. With clouded, old, wizened eyes he watched the fleeing girl's back, ramrod straight. He was at a loss how to handle the young woman now. In his mind's eye, he saw how she would entrance the crowd only hours ahead with her dazzling smiles and mystifying steps. He would devote the last ounce of what was left of his strength to make her shine. Already, in his mind's ear, he could hear the crowd roaring as the girl did wonders with her youthful body, dancing in a manner that showed the gods had her in mind when they created dance. In his mind's eye, he saw her sidestep this way like an antelope, and strut that way like a peacock, dancing as if she owned the copyright to dance. The man's heartbeat quickened as he pictured again the girl's breasts - young, round, supple, rising and falling in rhythm; the little nipples hard.

The man knew that in tonight's contest to choose the representative of the three villages in the regional dance contest coming up soon, the girl would win. He would be there to play for her, to make her shine, to make her the greatest dancer ever. The contest was only a matter of weeks, but it seemed like light years away. He couldn't wait. Raising his head, he was in time to see the girl, shoulders held high as she disappeared among a cluster of shrubs in the distance. He sighed, thinking, It wasn't my fault, what happened last time.

It was probably the millionth time the man had told himself this. He had tried to prevent it. But it was beyond his power. He knew the girl's grandmother was suspicious of his every move now. He would win the old woman's heart first and then…

I shouldn't have waited to chat with him, the girl thought as she hurried towards their village square, venue for the night's dance. He may begin to think that… The girl couldn't bring herself to say what the man may begin to think. She swallowed hard. It was painful. Apart from the shrill, but reassuring cries of crickets and an occasional chatter of bats overhead, there was no other sound to be heard except the steady beating of her heart, which resonated in her ears, and her light footsteps, which went, 'tap, tap, tap' on the dusty path.

The village square was rowdy, and buzzing with activities by the time the girl arrived. The moon was in full bloom. One could easily tell a grain of wheat from that of millet on the cold, sandy soil. As one amateur dancer left the dancing arena, another quickly commandeered it, showing off what she could do with her body, flexible like rubber. It would continue like this until after midnight when the actual contest would begin.

Everywhere, people mixed, freely. They ate roast meat, drank local tea brewed on miniature coal pots, chatted happily, the rigors of the farms and the daily struggle for survival on dug out canoes forgotten. Men and women, the old and the young teased each other. Everyone was lively. And lighthearted.

Every other month, the dance night was like this. The villagers looked forward to it: the men missing it terribly, the women longing for it. There were no restraints. Everyone mixed as he or she wished. Everyone shared freely with the other what he or she held sacrosanct.

Several days before these dance nights, the women took time off their routines of carrying and fetching, cooking and hoeing, grinding and weeding to preen themselves. They must look their best. Oil dripped from their hair, made into the latest fashion. Long rings adorned their ears. And noses. The soles of their feet and palms were decorated with dyes: red, indigo, yellow and other brilliant colors. Black too. On the actual dance nights, they wore expensive perfumes meant especially for the night. Every corner of the three villages was a garden with flowers in full bloom.

Alcohol made the dance days even more fun. The men folk who usually spent a greater portion of their day relaxing under tree shades, or visiting each other began drinking as soon as breakfast was over. One after the other, kegs and calabashes of palm wine were emptied. By evening, the men were truly soaked and ready for the dance. Just like their sweet smelling women folk.

The village square was big enough to house all the inhabitants of more than five villages for any occasion. As far as living memory could be relied on, the two-monthly dance among the three villages had always been held here. Huge silk-cotton, neem and mango trees, which formed a circle around the square ensured that no sandstorm, no matter how ferocious disturbed any events taking place in it. Wide, corrugated trunks provided enough crevices, deep enough to cheat the moon rays, especially on nights as this when the moon blazed away in glory.

Dinner over, inhabitants of the three villages began flocking to the dance venue. The mingling would then begin. Husbands and wives looked the other way when they saw their spouses engaged in gaily, sometimes hushed discussions with total strangers. As casual as possible, new partnerships were formed. Strolling hand in hand, the new partners found suitable places in and around the village square. There, their chitchats continued.

Every now and then, from somewhere in the dark, laughter rang out. Elsewhere, someone would smile knowingly, caressing the partner in response. Elsewhere still, some other person would giggle in ecstasy. This was how the inhabitants of the three villages, and even strangers from beyond would saturate all nooks and corners, until the climax of the night when the village maidens would cap it all with their tantalizing dances.

After the dance, those who weren't up to more gallivanting went home, to sleep off the effects of the night. The more adventurous, usually greater in number, found more intimate places to settle down.

Heaving and sweating bodies would litter the surrounding fields. One only needed to cough lightly, or shuffle his feet to disentangle entangled souls. It would be in the wee hours, as the dew began to descend and the temperature dropped before husbands saw wives, and wives husbands. Each would smile affectionately. Each would hug the other endearingly.

By daybreak, only the scintillating performances of the dancers occupied people's lips. During the coming days and weeks, partners of the dance night would run into each other. They would not acknowledge themselves.

At the end of each dance night, rather than lose herself like everyone else and partake in the night's fun, the girl was filled with revulsion as she watched admirers, some of whom they hardly know, lead her friends into the bowels of darkness. Especially she felt sour as women flocked around the man, praising him for his expertise on the saxophone; touching him here and touching him there, fondly. Always, the man got lured into the night. The girl would never see him until the next day. Or, several days later.

Not that she cared.

For the girl, this aspect of the night spoilt the beauty of her performance. It took away the joy that dancing brought. She was never able to regale at her achievement as the most gifted dancer in all the three villages. She didn't understand why things were like this.

When she was much younger and just perfecting her dance steps, she had taken the issue up with her grandmother.

"It is our tradition," her grandmother said. "It is our uniqueness."

"What," the girl said, "is our uniqueness?"

"To share," her grandmother answered. "To share with each other what we have."

"And that includes our bodies?" the girl said, cringing.

"It was like this during my mother's days."

"But grandmother, is it right? Can't one say no?"

"You are barely thirteen. Stop asking such questions. They will say I did not bring you up properly."

"But I want to know. Is it right, doing this thing?"

"There is nothing you or anybody can do about it. It is our way of life."

The girl, greatly repulsed shrank from her grandmother.

"Soon, I tell you my daughter," the grandmother said, "you will come to look forward to these nights, not because you want to dance but because you want to be free. Free to exercise your powers as a woman. Free to explore. I am old, doubly bent now and cannot partake in, as you call it, this 'thing' anymore, but in my days when I was as spry as you are now, possibly a bit older, I salivated for it."

"What?"

"My daughter, show me the person who can turn against his tradition, and I will hand the heavens to you as a reward."

Now sixteen, the girl was still amazed at this way of life, this tradition that gave no one the right to say, 'no'; this tradition that gave no one the right to cast away what was wrong, what was evil.

What would happen if she continued to think differently? Her friends, already indoctrinated were beginning to rib her. Could she, a mere girl, a mere woman, challenge custom?

As the girl stood there, thinking and surveying the crowd, she mentally sorted her steps. She knew she would win again tonight. It ailed her that she had no serious competitor in the three villages. It is just as well that the dance festival is coming up, she thought. With head held high, back straight, she strode determinedly past several young men. They were in the mood, which the night dictated. They catcalled her. The women called out too. Other girls who had come simply to have a go at what the night held afterwards whispered about her. She caught the envious glints in their painted, brown eyes. Other dancers called out to her. She did not respond. They let her be. She was in that trance-like mood which she fell into before every dance. Over the years, they had come to recognize it.

Her corner in the dressing area was empty. Untying her small bag, and with the help of the little girls who had gathered around her, the girl began to don her costume. She felt sorry for the innocent little girls. They didn't know yet what life held in store for them. They spoke to her. She answered with her smiles. She moved about as if possessed. Soon, she was lost again in her world of uncertainties. Thoughts about many things she didn't understand filled her mind. These many things hurt her. Like that time she had been cut. She was eleven years old then.

Slowly and vividly, the girl recalled her circumcision.

It was a terrible experience. One that she would never forget. Her cutting and that of a few other girls had been particularly traumatizing. By the time it got to their turn, the only knife being employed for the cutting had lost its sharpness, its cutting edge having been dulled by the congealed blood from the other girls, which lay thick on its rusted surface. Sharpening the knife on the piece of rock nearby only made the pain worse as the knife, now serrated, cut unevenly.

After the cutting, she had bled profusely. The palm oil and other concoctions derived from fluids expressed from various wild plants and fruits did nothing to alleviate her pain. If anything, the herbal applications worsened her condition. For days after, she was like the living dead. It was still a wonder that she had survived the severe bleeding and high fever, which accompanied the skin infection she had subsequently contracted. At the end of the day, though her damaged skin healed, it left behind a terrible scar, an ugly streak of pink.

The girl knew she would never get over this scar.

Once in a while she still experienced terrible pains from this scar, especially when she danced so hard or walked long distances or did any hard work on the farm.

"It was the same with me and with your mother and all other women of our tribe," her grandmother had consoled. "We all went through these same rites of passage. That is what makes a woman a woman. The pain will come and go but eventually you will outgrow it. It is the pain of womanhood. It is what prepares you for the uncertainties of time."

For the girl, over time, this 'Pain of Womanhood', has changed its nature, assuming newer dimensions. It was now a psychological torture; a 'Pain of Shame'. She felt humiliated and cheated by the act. She felt violated, debased. It was her body. Was it not rightly her place to say 'no' or 'yes' to whatever anyone wanted to do to it? What if she had died from the infection she contracted? What if she had caught this new disease people got by sharing knives and needles? Now that they had severed her sensitive parts, what if she never enjoyed sex? Who would shoulder the blame if it turned out that she never got pregnant? Who would shoulder the blame when due to lack of a child she became a pariah in society?

The magical sound of a saxophone suddenly floated over to the girl, rousing her from her deep thoughts. She was surprised to note that she had completed dressing. Judging from the time it usually took under normal circumstances, it meant that her mind had been roaming the past for upwards of half an hour. She sighed regrettably as the memories receded from her brain. She knew they would come back to haunt her before the night was over.

Looking up, she saw that the other dancers were bent double in the dancing arena, rocking steadily to the soothing melody of the saxophone which rose and fell, rose and fell as if coming from a far, far distance on the back of a gentle wind. She did not have to strain herself to see who was playing. The quality of the sound was all too familiar. In a moment she sprang to her feet like an agitated tigress. The crowd roared as they discovered who had come to tease them.

Gingerly, she approached the man, as a lioness would stalk an antelope it was sure to have for dinner. She beckoned him with her hands, teased and dazzled him with her smiles. She rolled her tongue at him and her full waist rocked left and right; up and down. The sound of the vibrating metallic bangles on her ankles and wrists blended perfectly with the drums and flutes, now accompanying the saxophone.

The girl was soon lost in her art. As she wove this way and that, the frenzied crowd went crazy, lending their clapping to the sounds of the musical instruments. The night came alive, pulsating like an angry monster as the ground shook with the stamping of thousands of excited feet. Everything else blurred into oblivion for the girl. Two other dancers, now joining in tried to divert attention from the girl, but it was impossible to tear one's eyes from the girl once she was dancing, hypnotized by the magical sounds of the man's saxophone.

The girl's eyes locked with the man's eyes briefly as she raised her head to beckon to the gods of music and dance, far away and watching in the bright starry sky. And the man saw her smile, saw her flirt with him... just fleetingly and his cleft lip parted in a gentle smile and the loneliness which resided in his heart skipped away, albeit temporarily and he knew instant happiness; knew instant bliss. With his mind's palms, he clutched her smile firmly, burying it in the recess of his being. These nights... these dancing nights, when the girl danced for him, he thought. How he longed for them.

Shaking his head wildly, as if delirious, the frail, old man threw himself into his saxophone, prepared to play out his soul. Cradling his saxophone to his chest, he limped about like a monkey, unconscious of the giggles his acrobatics drew. The dancing was approaching its crescendo when suddenly the girl halted in mid action, lost steam and went limp.

No.

She would save her best for last.

The crowd sighed. Hungrily. The girl had strung them so tight and had released them without warning. Stepping back and wiping the sweat off their foreheads, they exhaled deeply. They couldn't wait for the real thing later.

Just as she had entered, the girl exited the arena. Children crowded her, chants in her praise filling the dusty night air.

Hobbling away, the man retired under an old neem tree to wipe perspiration off his brow and get back his breath. He collapsed on the dry wood of one of several buttress roots, which had since lost their fleshy coverings due to over usage by both humans and beasts. Taking out a piece of cloth from his shirt pocket, he painstakingly wiped the mouthparts of his saxophone, after first wiping the sides of his own mouth which was crusted with saliva. All the while, he thought about the girl. One moment she was all tensed up, and wouldn't utter a single word to him. The next she was as willing as a wily cat. She confused him. In fact, he still blamed her for everything. His hands shook and a ripple went through him as he recalled their shame.

Slowly the night progressed. Midnight came and went. When the dance finally ended hours later and the man, alone and lonely, and unable to stop himself, tried to lure the girl away into the blackness, the moon having gone to bed, all he got was a face loaded with questions. Questions he had no answers to. He didn't press her, thinking, Soon, out of her own volition she will come around. She has no choice in the matter. The man knew that like all other women of the three villages, the girl was trapped. She was trapped in the ways prescribed by custom and tradition. Only she didn't know it. The man felt sorry for the girl. And for himself too.

the road farer

It was approaching 7pm. Still the central motor park in Onitsha was a cacophony of sounds, with hawkers ululating at the top of their tested voices as they called attention to their sun-bleached wares; and conductors locked in fierce, unending battle for passengers, hollering, '*Ochanjá*', 'Main market', 'Central hospital', 'Police line', 'Water side', and the names of other commercial and residential areas in guttural, marijuana tampered voices.

However, it was the simultaneous loud honking and blaring of the numerous *Gwongworo* horns that brought Okon slowly awake. He had been asleep for nearly six hours! Okon was a popular *Gwongworo* driver. Anyone who swore he hadn't set eyes on him before must definitely have seen his 12-wheeled, heavy duty, 'Man Diesel' lorry. His philosophy, '*No paddy for jungle,*' which was also his nickname was splashed with red and yellow paint all over the wooden body of his *Gwongworo*. It was done in such calligraphy that you would be blind not to notice it.

Remembering the circumstances surrounding his lengthy sleep, Okon allowed a gentle smile to play across his wrinkled face, dry as a lizard's back. *Ha!* All his life road faring, he had never experienced anything like it. He felt as if his whole body had been panel-beated. Or put through a wringer! The '*Omoge*' was simply incredible, he thought. Why, she had done such nice things to him, and taken him to such heights he believed existed only in fairy tales. Funny, because she didn't look like a pleasure worker. And the more he thought about it, the more he disagreed with himself that she was one.

"Anyway," he surmised, aching his eyebrows and furiously scraping his left collar bone with long nails, heavily laden underneath with dirt, "wit all de poverty for town, and de longthroat of woman of nowadays, no person can able to separate de chaff from de grains."

The truth of the matter was that Okon didn't really care which she was: chaff or grain. What in fact mattered to him was his fun. He never joked with it.

Cash was no barrier.

** **

Okon was indeed proud of himself. It was by obeying his sixth sense that he had won the woman in question, whom he now regarded as his 'jackpot'. Earlier in the day, on his way from Abakaliki, she had flagged him down by Ogbor hills, shouting:

"Onitsha...Onitsha...Onitsha...sir, you dey go Onitsha?"

Having jogged all the way, she was a little breathless by the time she met him where he had screeched to a stop, barely off the highway. She was tall. Darker than any human being he had seen before, Okon knew, even without first feeling it, that her skin was smoother than a babe's. And time would prove him right! As he watched, the charcoal black skin glittered, and bounced off sunrays, separating them neatly into the colours of the rainbow! Okon knew it was the handiwork of oil extracted from snakeskin. Only it could have such mesmerizing effect when rubbed on the body.

Okon could hardly believe his luck, and sighed longingly as he surveyed her geography, drinking the elements of her gargantuan feature. Her chest, which rose and fell rhythmically, was filled to the brim and overflowing, he noticed. And her backside? Okon simply had no description for that, a wonder, because by his nature, there was nothing that he could not nail an appropriate description to. One thing was sure though: given the chance, he could rest his large head on the gaping cleavage of that chest or the mound of that backside for eternity.

She was a handful, just the way he likes his women, Okon told himself. Why, he wasn't in that league of men who messed about with skinny folks who soon got lost in a large divan. But then, that was Okon for you! This very Okon had in the past been known to make a solid, solid case for the so-called 'skinny folks'. Truth was that he wasn't particularly certain which he preferred: skinny folks or handfuls! It all depended on what fate dished in his plate...like this accidental encounter.

As he sat contemplating the mass, dressed in sparkling white '*buba* and wrapper,' with a matching headgear, who now gazed up at him, Okon swore:

"Even if I no dey go Onitsha, for dis fine Omoge, I go face dat direction right now."

As if reading his mind about heading to Onitsha even if that were not his original destination, she smiled. Okon's heart tumbled severally, thrashing wildly as he took in the beautiful gap in the middle of her upper denture. His throat ran instantly dry and every time he opened his mouth, words eluded him, like the answer to the Devil's puzzle. All he could do was lean across and hold the passenger's door open and, nodding his head repeatedly, bade her to step aboard.

"Bassey, make space for de lady," he managed to croak at his conductor, seated beside him at last. "Go stay for back small," he continued. "As gentleman, you know say na ladies first."

Okon was smiling broadly now. Bassey was not impressed with his master's sudden etiquette. He knew the man well. Why, Okon respected neither king nor clergy.

And Bassey protested.

"But Oga, space plenty here for me and de lady."

Okon's smile faded instantly and his eyes flashed fire. But checking his anger, he replied calmly: "Stupid fool. Do as I tell you quick, quick." He did not want to upset his fair fare.

Bassey needed no further urging. Giving his master a knowing wink (for this was not the first time), he jumped down deftly and made for the back of the lorry.

The rest had been routine job for Okon. After all these years of road faring, he was adept at it now. He could, if given enough time talk his way into even Jezebel's cold heart.

And he had had enough time. Onitsha was a good three hours drive away.

** **

Recalling his 'jackpot's' great body, Okon emitted a long groan of desire. He then groped for her in the now darkened room. His wandering hands encountered empty space. He was surprised that she was not in the bed with him, and he got up with a start. Then he heard water running softly in the bathroom.

"Ahhh, she dey freshen up," he thought gaily, "_and no better place to wack dis sweet honey pot again than for bathroom?"

An interesting copulating position crossed his mind and his heart danced to an imaginary *rub-a-dub.*

"Na from back I go do am dis time," he assured himself, smiling mischievously. "She go know say she jam strong man today."

Even at fifty-five years, Okon was still as strong as a bull. The ripples of muscle on his flanks and biceps attested to this. You couldn't be a driver who steered a powerful lorry day after day without being well endowed muscularly. Picking his way gingerly with the aid of the dying rays of the

133

setting sun, which streamed in through cracks in the window, he staggered to the bathroom, naked. His potbelly preceded him. Opening the bathroom door excitedly, his rising erection went limp.

His fair lady was not there either.

Ha!

He rushed to the door. It was locked, with the only key firmly latched in the keyhole! The realization that she was gone hit him with all the force of a falling wave. His heart fluttered and spluttered and puffed, like an old locomotive as alarm overtook him.

"Chei, I don die!" he cried out loud. "She don carry my money disappear. Oh Jehovah God, my own don finish!"

Searching frantically, with his potbelly obstructing him most of the time, he found his Berec torchlight. He soon discovered that his wallet, which contained his earnings for the past week, was safe. He had hidden it expertly between some cracks in the wall, where not even a money detector could have sniffed it out. Okon praised his ingenuity, thinking:

"Wit ladies of nowadays, person get to careful well, well."

Looking around with the aid of the torchlight, he located a candle stand containing a partially used candle and a matchbox. In a moment, the dingy motel room came alive. Scattered everywhere were articles of *their* clothing.

Ha!

"Or she go away naked?" he wondered aloud in bewilderment.

Recalling the small holdall she was carrying, Okon concluded that she must have changed into something new before departing.

"But why she left her clothes dem behind? Dis one is queer," he surmised, and the leathery skin of his dry face squeezed in vain glory. It was not often such exotic words as 'queer' stole into his slim vocabulary. "And she no even ask for money. Or she be Mother Christmas?"

Maybe she will come back, Okon thought. Too bad she wouldn't meet him then, but then tomorrow was another day, he consoled. After all, she now knew where to find him.

Rummaging through the rubble, he reached for his white Hinge's underwear. It was not there. Neither were her own underwear. It appeared both were the only items she had taken along with her.

Ha!

To make assurance doubly sure, he searched under the bed, in the cupboards, in the bathroom.

Nothing.

Ha!

"Na wetin be de meaning of all dis?" he asked no one in particular.

"Why she go disappear wit my pant. Maybe she wear de thing join her own by mistake," he tried to explain to himself, but soon discarded the implausible hypothesis.

"Or she wan take am do juju?" he wondered, but soon discarded this line of thinking too. Okon considered himself a good Christian, and did not believe in jujus. So, why would she go away with his underpants? Not finding a suitable answer, he headed back to the bathroom to clear his body of her grim. Several minutes later, he stepped out refreshed. A peek at his weather worn wristwatch lying on the bedside table revealed that soon, it would be 8 o'clock. Any moment from now, Chief Agbaka would arrive with his entourage. The irritable chief had hired Okon for a round trip to Abakaliki to haul 300 bags of rice. Okon was determined not to be the cause of any delays, for, apart from the fact that Abakaliki was a whole night's journey, Chief Agbaka had, from the day he hired the lorry indicated his desire to depart early.

Quickly, he got dressed.

"Well, na small world be dis," Okon philosophised, as he threw on the last of his clothes. "Somehow, we go meet again if God talk so."

And with this thought of their meeting again if providence so decreed, Okon instantly forgot everything about the mysterious lady. It never crossed his mind to wonder how she had unlocked the room, stepped out and then relocked it, with the key still latched on the keyhole within! Neither did the whereabouts of his white Hinge's underwear worry him any further, especially considering the fact that it was torn on one side and he had been meaning to discard it anyway.

** **

One tiny inconvenience led to another, and another led to another. At last, 'African time' prevailed and to Chief Agbaka's irritation, they began the journey much, much later than planned. Now, it was about 3 o'clock in the morning and they had been travelling for nearly four hours. The moon was shining brightly. From a distance, Okon glimpsed the silhouette of Ogbor hills. In the darkness of his driver's cabin, he allowed himself a faint smile. The towering hills reminded him of his morning's conquest.

In that brief moment it took Okon to cast his mind back to his escapades of the morning before, he lost control of his *Gwongworo*. The lorry veered off dangerously into the forest. Okon struggled to rein it in, barely succeeding. Suddenly, a loud explosion shattered the silence of the night, bringing the lorry to an abrupt halt. All occupants of the lorry woke up with violent starts, each fearing for his life.

135

For the ill-tempered Chief Agbaka, already aggravated by the late take off, the issue of his safety was the least of his concern. On hearing the explosion, he clutched the polyethylene bag he held to his chest tighter, his bony fingers aching. The bag contained his entire retirement benefit. Chief Agbaka who had only just retired from the government service was venturing into business for the first time. With heart quaking, he waited for the command from the armed robbers and was ready to die rather than watch them cart away his insurance for old age. When the command did not come, he asked with a quivering voice:

"What happened?"

No answer was forthcoming. His confidence grew.

"I say what is happening?" He repeated.

"The lorry enter forest by mistake, Chief. Na just the tire burst," Bassey the conductor replied.

The relief the old Chief felt on discovering that his money was safe after all was too immense, but this was soon overshadowed as irate anger overtook him. He released several hard questions into the air, without waiting for a single answer.

"How manage? ...I say where is Okon? ...My man Mr. *Gwongworo* driver, were you sleeping and dreaming useless dreams? Or drunk? I thought you were an experienced driver ...Look, if I am late getting to Abakaliki, it would be better a boa constrictor or a python swallowed you whole."

Everybody laughed heartily, except Chief Agbaka.

"Chief take am easy," Okon consoled, laughing as he clasped Chief Agbaka on the shoulder. "It is not a heavy problem. I have very, very sound spare, and we go soon be on our way again. Bassey, fix dat tire fast and good, you hear me?"

"But you trust me, Oga-"

"Forget about whether I trust you or not. Just fix de tire, dat is what I want."

Bassey set to work changing the punctured tire.

After a short while, Okon yawned loudly and announced:

"Let me step inside the forest for a while and relieve myself."

"No problem Oga."

Amid the snapping protest of dry twigs and leaves as he laid his over one hundred kilos squarely on them, Okon's snaked his way into the nearby forest. He had overfed himself at dinnertime with pounded yam and a delicious mix of three-part bitter-leaf soup and one-part *egusi* soup, all in an attempt to regain the vast energy he had expended on his 'jackpot'.

He had first felt nature's call at the motor park, but had suppressed it because Chief Agbaka was screaming blue murder about how late they were, and heaping all the blame squarely on him, even though he had no part in making them late. And all the while he drove, he still had that urge and had been looking for a good enough reason to stop. Thanks to the sudden explosion of the lorry tire. He could now take all the time in the world while his conductor fixed the 'friendly' tire.

Okon shone his torch here and there as he weaved his way among tree stumps and twigs and shrubs. The light was a fading yellow. He made a mental note to change the batteries when he arrived Abakaliki.

His ears soon caught faint chanting from the direction of the highway, a confirmation that Bassey was hard at work. Bassey always chanted whenever he was changing a punctured tire or assisting the mechanics drop the old lorry's engine. He liked Bassey. Powerfully built, the young man was a workhorse. At eighteen, he could single-handedly change all the wheels of any lorry in no time. Okon knew that the glowing moon up in the heavens would make the work seem like child's play to Bassey. He knew he must hurry. After moving several meters, he decided he had gone far enough. Finally selecting a nice spot, he set about emptying his congested bowels, after shining his dying Berec torch here and there to make sure he was not in a lion's den. The dying rays from the torch fell on a piece of white clothing near by, but Okon was too pressed to take any notice. Finally discharging a gigantic load of faecal matter, he felt better. Contentedly now, he resumed his little detective work with his torch. Then the yellowish rays fell on the piece of white clothing again.

This time, Okon took notice.

** **

Forty-five minutes later, Bassey hitched up his three quarter jean trousers held in place by a synthetic twine, and emerged from under the lorry.

"Chief," he called out, "I don fix de tire."

Chief Agbaka was a man who was used to sound night sleep. As soon as he got reassured that he was not under attack by armed robbers and that his retirement benefit was safe, he went back inside the lorry to await the fixing of the blown tire. He had instantly fallen asleep, his black polyethylene bag clutched tenaciously to his chest.

"Chief," Bassey called, shaking him gently awake, " I don fix de tire."

The old man woke with a violent start, clutching his polyethylene bag even tighter, and gasping breathlessly:

"*Ego mu O*...my money O."

Bassey smiled to himself, thinking how easy it would be to knock off the old man and disappear with all that money meant for 300 bags of the stony Abakaliki rice.

"I say de tire don okay now," he announced again.

"Then let us proceed, what are we waiting for?" a relieved Chief Agbaka cried.

"My Oga..."

"What is wrong with your master?"

"He never come back from the forest."

"Which forest?"

"He go obey nature."

"Then go and fetch him, and be quick about it!"

"I no know which way he go," Bassey lied.

"He go dat way," Chief Agbaka's three handymen chorused, pointing in the dark.

The trio had suddenly materialized from the shadows where they had been lazing away while Bassey, alone, laboured under the lorry. Bassey eyed them, thinking to give them a piece of his mind, but decided to wait for a more appropriate time.

"I say go and look for him, Mr Conductor," Chief Agbaka barked, his voice carrying into the distance.

"He go soon come back, so let's wait. Meanwhile, everybody make sure you no left anything behind," Bassey commanded.

** **

And they began to wait.

** **

Thirty minutes came and went.

An hour came and went.

And still, Okon the *Gwongworo* driver was nowhere to be seen. He had been away for over two hours!

Everyone was visibly worried now.

"Maybe he dey born pikin inside forest", one of Chief Agbaka's boys joked but no one laughed at this silly joke of Okon being in labour inside the forest.

"Maybe he really was slumbering. That explains why the lorry went off the road. Has he by chance fallen asleep in the forest while defecating?" Chief Agbaka queried.

Somewhere in the distance, a cock crowed.

"Or has he missed his way and wandered off in another direction?" Chief Agbaka moaned after a while, and then began to rant:

"Unbelievable! _Unbelievable! How can a full-grown man like Okon not find his way back from this godforsaken forest, eh? How?"

"Let us go into the forest and search for him," Bassey suggested.

Since the fact that his boss might be missing was becoming a reality, he had been the least vocal, being thoroughly embarrassed by the big man's behaviour. He wondered what magic could be keeping him enthralled in the forest. When no one bothered to respond to his suggestion of, 'Let us go into the forest and search for him', Bassey repeated it.

"Your suggestion is well noted, but you go and search for him alone, after all, he is your lord and master," came the sharp retort from Chief Agbaka. "As for me and these young men here, we are not stepping an inch into this thick forest. Never."

Bassey shrugged his heavy shoulders in resignation. Soon it would be morning anyway. If by then his master had still not materialised, then the villagers residing around Ogbor hills could be enlisted to help search for him.

** **

Three hours later, the events of the night as they occurred was narrated to villagers on their way to their farms, and to the weekly market in the neighbouring village. Not one of them agreed to set foot into the forest of Ogbor hills without first being able to tell a palm frond from a coconut frond. As more and more of them arrived to the scene, each wanted to know what had happened, and the story was retold, every new attempt more flavoured than the last, and told with a perfect melodrama.

"He just go yonder to clear his throat," Bassey would begin. "Den he go down small to piss."

"Eeehe," would come the unanimous reply as the villagers urged him on.

"De nex thing he tell us is that..."

"He was not telling us. How many times will I correct you this useless conductor?" And Chief Agbaka would take up the story line. "Gentlemen, I was dozing inside the front seat when I heard him telling his conductor here, 'not us' as the useless boy now claims that he was going to relieve himself inside the forest."

"And by what time was this?" one of the first villagers to arrive would ask again for the benefit of the new comers.

"It was well after three O' clock."

"Three O'clock?" would come the consternated chorus.

"Yes, three O' clock," Bassey would confirm, shamefaced.

"But this man, what did you people say is his name again?"

"Okon, Joshua Okon-"

"Okay, Joshua Okon. Couldn't this Joshua Okon have relieved himself around here? I mean is there a lady amongst you?"

"Even if there was a woman, or women amongst us," barked Chief Agbaka. "What is Okon carrying between his legs that a woman has not set eyes on before? *Ibi*, eh?...Hernia?"

"Didn't this Okon know that Ogbor hills is a very dangerous place to venture into in the cover of darkness?" one villager, just arriving asked. "You can find all kinds and manner of creatures within, including wild animals like lion and tiger, *mmo*...evil spirits, and even rebels!"

At the mention of 'rebels', everyone smiled despite the seriousness of the matter. Even Chief Agbaka. No matter how he tried, he could not kill the smile that sprouted on his robust cheeks.

And the questions continued raining, like enemy bullets.

"Is he new on this road, this Joshua Okon?" someone wanted to know.

Poor Bassey. He was close to tears now, but he knew the onus was on him to defend his master's integrity, which the no-nonsense Chief Agbaka was intent on defaming. "No," he replied. "My Oga don dey ply dis route since de last millennium. Before den, him na conductor for nearly ten years, before den..."

"Enough of his godforsaken life history," Chief Agbaka roared. "Let's just pray we find him alive. I will then teach him a lesson not to mess around with me, Chief Remigus Agbaka."

Everyone stared at Chief Agbaka's whiskers as it twitched this way and that and his prominent Adam's apple, stone-like on an elongated neck, wobbled up and down. The old man, even in his wildest imagination could not have contemplated such as terribly botched business trip. Like a leaf under the influence of an angry wind, he shook violently with anger.

"Gentlemen, we all know that this *ifa*..this story telling, enthralling as it is will do us no good," one of the villagers, an austere man with sharp, penetrating eyes finally advised. "Instead we must concentrate our minds and energies on locating this lorry driver."

Everyone agreed he had spoken well.

"Which way did you people say he went?" the man asked.

"Dat way," Bassey answered pointing, at the same time blowing his nose and increasing the pressure on the synthetic twine that served as his belt.

After a tense minute of heated deliberation, the villagers decided it was light enough to go searching for the missing lorry driver. Not only could they tell a palm from a coconut frond now, they would, if the case arose, see exactly what direction to disappear to, and save themselves untimely death. From nondescript parts of their bags, out came cutlasses of various shapes and sizes. For weaponry, Bassey the conductor, Chief Agbaka and his entourage made do with tree branches and stones lying by the roadside.

"We will have to divide ourselves into two search groups," the austere man commanded. From the way he talked, it was clear he was a man used to giving orders and being obeyed. Nobody argued with him.

"Mr Conductor, you, you, you, you, you, you and you," he said, pointing at each man one after the other, you will go this way, he said pointing to the north. "You, Chief, Chief... you, you, you, you, you, Mazi Ijene, Uncle Iloje, you, you and myself," we will take up the search from this area, he said pointing to the point where it was supposed that Okon entered the forest. "If any group should see anything suspicious, whistle, and we will all converge at that point and then take the lead from there. Do we understand each other?"

"Yes," came the chorus.

"Any questions?"

There were no questions, and the groups broke up and made to go their separate ways, when the austere man halted them.

"Mr Conductor, you will lead the first group and Chief...Chief... here will lead our group."

"I will rather not," Chief Agbaka protested with a vehement shake of his head and a furious wagging of one finger. His reason? He wanted to give the younger generation a chance! A chance for what, no one knew. But none ventured to ask for clarification for fear of being spat at, what with the way Chief Agbaka had his mouth pouted, like a cobra, eager to spit venom. Even the austere man maintained a sealed lip.

They had not been in the forest longer than a few minutes when Bassey's group stumbled upon a most bizarre scene and raised an ear splitting alarm. Moments later, the other group, like a bunch of drunkards came tearing and stumbling through the undergrowth. With hearts pounding, muscles tensing and neck veins pulsating dangerously, every one gaped open mouthed at the macabre scene.

** **

Remember that Okon had been playing Sherlock Holmes with his torchlight? Well, the sight that had caught his eyes was that of a squeezed underwear carelessly thrown aside. He smiled to himself as the possible circumstances surrounding the abandoning of this underwear, right in the middle of the forest crossed his mind. He imagined a desperate passenger scampering off, forgetting it as the vehicle in which he was travelling threatened to leave him behind. He could not help but giggle now. He himself had, uncountable times in the past played this expensive joke on unsuspecting passengers.

With a dry twig, he dragged the piece of underclothing nearer, enjoying his mock play at detective. Spreading it, he proceeded to examine it further with the dull light from his torch, like a forensic pathologist. It was a Hinge brand, he noticed. Something about it was vaguely familiar ...the little tear on the side ... and then he froze as recognition hit him. Lo and behold, it was his Hinge underwear! The very one on which account he had turned the dingy motel room upside down and not found. His mind whirled around in turmoil as a cold prickle stabbed his stomach.

"But how? How it take reach here?" he shouted, unaware he was doing so. His hands shook miserably and sweat broke out all over his body, despite the cool atmosphere of the forest at this time of the day. A gentle wind suddenly began to blow, deepening his *deja vu.* His heart thundered within his ribs, the sound echoing in his ears. Panicked, he jumped away from his excrement, not wishing to step on it, but finding his right leg sinking into it nonetheless. Not caring, he began buttoning up his trousers speedily. And then, giant goose pimples over ran his entire body.

He had company!

"Na who be dat?" he asked, exercising his arrogance. But it was only a whisper. Taking a deep breath, he cleared his throat as best as he could, and asked again:

"I say na who be dat?"

It was then he felt the slithering mass surround him as leaves and twigs rattled and rustled. What ever it was, Okon knew it was huge, what with the way the ground shook. As he opened his mouth to scream, a force of several horsepower struck him at the nape, stunning him. He fell like a log, kicking and struggling and agonisingly flinging his shoes and cap and Berec torchlight hither thither.

** **

It was this paraphernalia of personal effects, and a mess of excrement, already commandeered by buzzing, giant green forest flies that the search party now gazed upon. Bassey was quick to identify the personal effects as belongings to his master.

"Are you sure they are his?" Chief Agbaka asked, clearly distressed.

"Yes Chief, I sure, na my Oga get all dis things wey scatter here so," Bassey answered.

"But where is the Okon then?" Chief Agbaka cried.

"I think he ran off when something attacked him," one of the villagers volunteered.

"What can it be that attacked and frightened off a full grown man like Okon?" Chief Agbaka asked. You could hear the tremor in his voice.

"How can anyone be certain without further investigations?" the austere man answered.

"Folks, do you people seriously think it is safe to continue this further investigation?" Chief Agbaka whined, exhibiting that his feminine character for which his wife had always chided him.

"He may be hiding somewhere, needing help or he may be seriously wounded and any intervention now could be what is needed to save him," another villager hypothesized.

"Couldn't some of us go back to the lorry in case he turns up there? He may need help if he does. I volunteer to do that." As he spoke, his voice and hands and legs shook, and the polyethylene bag, clutched tightly against his chest vibrated. His eyes, crystal clear, darted this way and that like a rat's, cornered at last by a notorious alley cat.

"Thank you very, very much for volunteering, Chief, but if my master no show up last night, he no go show up now," Bassey said emphatically as he realised that Chief Agbaka was in the final stages of persuading the villagers to abandon the search for his master. "As one party, I suggest say make we all proceed with dis search."

Though the majority of the villagers would have loved to toe Chief Agbaka's line, no one said so, not wanting to look womanly before their contemporaries and the brave, young conductor, especially at this crucial time when they were required to prove their valour as men, something they boasted about to their children and wives virtually every passing day.

** **

Nerves were taut now, nearing snapping point. But then, were they not men? Some of them even had two chieftaincy titles. And so as one body, they advanced determinedly in search of the lorry driver. They followed the clear trail left behind by whatever had aggressed the good lorry driver, forcing him to kick off his shoes and leave his cap and torchlight (his fateful companion) behind.

For twenty minutes they followed cautiously, examining a broken twig here; a red paste resembling blood there; a footprint here; a brown matter smelling like excrement there. The trail led tortuously to one of the caves stowed safely away in the foot of Ogbor hills. Chief Agbaka, short and stout and still determined to give the younger generation a chance clearly preferred to lead the rear, letting Bassey and others take the front.

The search team was not to be disappointed. Just at the entrance of the cave was the object of their search. Its multicolour, which would make the rainbow jealous, glistered and reflected wondrously in the early morning sun. Everyone noticed its midsection:

It was clearly distended!

As to the content of this midsection, no one was in doubt!

The reptile was in the final process of manoeuvring into the bowels of the cave when the approaching men suddenly startled it. Seeing them on raising its head, with bifurcated tongues flickering this way and that, it heaved its massive body in one final movement to disappear into the cave.

Thinking it was gunning for them, the search party scattered in all directions, every man for himself.

One never saw such a stampede before.

Machetes, sticks, stones and other weaponry were flung far and wide as the men scampered, manly valour dashed through the window. As Chief Agbaka fled, with polyethylene bag clutched tightly against his chest and muffled wails escaping his parched throat, he regretted not heeding his dear wife's advice of leaving this Abakaliki rice business for the younger men, and finding something less risky in Onitsha to invest his retirement benefit on.

** **

Later when the police arrived from the divisional headquarters in Awka, armed to the teeth, and intent on recovering the remains of Okon the lorry driver, no sign of the creature was to be seen anywhere. Not even after tear-gassing the cave and sending a special squad to probe its dark interior. All they could do was add a white Hinge underwear, with a little tear at the side to the assortment of personal belongings found at the site where the lorry driver was thought to have been licked and swallowed. These they took for Mrs. Njide Okon, wife of the lorry driver for identification.

As to the identity of the huge reptile, the search party failed to reach a consensus. While Chief Agbaka thought it was a female *African rock python*, Bassey the conductor was convinced, it was a male *boa constrictor,* even though he had never, in his entire life set eyes on a boa constrictor, either male or female. To prove his conviction, Bassey, un-coaxed, swore by his grandmother's grave.

The End.

i remember Syl and other stories

waiting for the ferry

It is another evening. Dusk has settled on the motor park outside the ferry terminal. The cacophony has died down, the dust has settled on stalls and cars; clothes and buildings and trees, coating everything. In the distance, I can hear a hawker's voice, clear, crisp. "Buy my bread. Buy my hot sweet bread." I know how soft, and sometimes crunchy, those breads can be when hot. I imagine the light brown loaves, wrapped in shreds of flour paper, well salted, kind to the taste buds. My Adams apple slides up and down.

The sea waves thunder as they crash on the shore, dissipating their energies, wasting, dying. I peer afar, trying to figure out where the shore begins. I can only make out an undulating greenish mass, heaving, breathing, heavy, unending. Still further afar my eyes search. The town across the sea lies as if dead. Its electric lights look dejected, as they stand isolated from each other. It is the ferry I am searching for. I am unable to make out its form. It may still be picking up passengers and goods on the other end, I think. I settle down, prepared to wait. I hope the ferry comes early. I do not have the heart to spend another night here by the motor park outside the ferry terminal. But as my wristwatch, oblivious to my deepest worries, ticks away, that prospect seems more and more likely. I am afraid. The queue of vehicles and trucks waiting to board the ferry stretches as far as the eyes can see. And I am still a long way from the middle. I do not have a bright chance.

I am seated at the same spot as last time: on the broken bench supported at either ends by slabs of stone in front of the roast meat shop. I watch the goings on inside the meat shop with disinterest: lumps of mutton hanging on ropes firmly tied to the blackened ceiling swing slightly; the meat seller and his apprentice busy at their respective tasks. The meat seller, with a dirty apron (torn everywhere except at the pockets) hanging lopsidedly from his thick neck, flowing across a rounded stomach is waiting on a prospective client, his first for the night. The client, a fellow traveller waiting for the ferry is a tall man in the habit of constantly flattening his moustache with his left hand, his right hand out of sight behind his back. My co-traveller points to a not too big chunk of meat, swaying slightly at the ends of a rope. The meat seller is happy to hang the chunk down. I prepare to listen.

"How much?"

"It is half kilo, probably more."

The meat seller is in a hurry. He drops the meat into a weighing pan by a battery charged fluorescent lamp. The light is poor. I watch the scale's pointer as it trembles violently, then rests somewhere. That must be the half-kilo mark, I think.

"How much?" my co-traveller repeats.

"Seventy-five only."

"Seventy what? It is only fat and oil, little or no meat."

He extricates his right hand from behind his back, pokes and prods the chunk of fat on the weighing machine here and there. The meat seller is patient.

"We sell by weight," the meat seller says. "Not by body parts."

"So how much is that liver hanging over there?" my co-traveller asks.

I follow the direction of his fingers. The liver, dull red, hangs majestically from a nail point on the wall. It is a choice part.

"Livers are sold differently," the meat seller says. " How much do you want to pay for the fat and oil?"

My co-traveller walks out of the shop; his eyes jam mine. He smiles. I lower my head. I am embarrassed by his action, so vile; so wicked.

I notice the dog. Its tail is lowered. Its nose is to the ground. Its fur is frazzled. Its breast flap to the left and to the right as it trots. The breasts are heavy. Just probably littered, I think. Coming from feeding its puppies. Probably hungry and looking for something to eat, then go back to breastfeeding its young. I follow it with my eyes and locate the position of the bin. It snoops at the base. Nothing there to be picked up and guzzled. It raises itself on hind legs, looks into the bin. It then jumps down. Nothing there either, I think. Raising its head, it looks expectantly in the direction of the roast meat shop. The meat seller is busy cutting up meat for a new client. The dog is alert. Its tongue flick out a few times and lick its lips. The meat seller extracts some chunks of bones and slimy part from the portion he is cutting up. He bundles them up as to form a round lump that fits into his palm. He makes to throw the lump through the door to the bin, but he sights the dog. He then throws the lump into the roaring fire, which his apprentice has got going. The slime and bone sizzles and burns, letting off sparks and greenish and bluish flame. The dog and I watch the lump burn into ashes, a low whine reaching me from the direction of the dog. Turning, the dog ambles away, its watery eyes sad. I watch it go. I am sad too. Such thoughtlessness!

Odour of frying onions rouses me out of a disturbing reverie. It is cold now. I hug myself tight. I swallow hard as saliva rush to my mouth. The smell of roast meat is overpowering. Maybe I should call for some, I think. I pat my breast pocket. Then change my mind when I remember the dog. Three clients are inside the roast meat shop, in a special alcove. How come I didn't see them come in? I think. They are shovelling meat and onions into their mouths and minding their businesses, not talking to each other. I watch them as they chew tentatively, meditatively and then swallow. I swallow with them. They are men in their late forties, early fifties; the sort with three or more wives and a horde of children. I become them. We chew together, swallow together, pick up the next lump of meat together, savour the sweetness together, our eyes blank. We lick our fingers together, one finger after the other, smack our lips in unison. I know men like these. In an hour's time or thereabouts, these men will be home to their wives. They will reject dinner, citing various reasons, from too much salt to excess pepper to the food being cold, bland, tasteless, fit only for beasts. They will pick up quarrels with their wives, and then beat them silly, with their children screaming off their heads as they defend their helpless mothers. What nonsense, the men would demand. They would then enumerate their glorious deeds, ticking them one after the other on their fingers: how they have slaved since morning on dug out canoes, or under the sun in market places, or in the farms planting yams or digging up cassava. How when they wish to come home to a tasty meal, all they get is cold, over-salted food fit only for slaves. How they aren't dogs.

One after the other, the men finish their meat, crack the bones, clean the plates, wash everything down with a bottle of Coke, or Fanta. The meat seller has a gas-operated fridge, blackened by smoke, by a corner. The apprentice moves away the plastic plates quickly. One after the other, the men rise and leave, belching in my face as they pass, their breaths laden with mustard and curry and onions. Other roast meat lovers come in to take their place, paying no attention to me as they pass. I am deep in thought as I watch the newcomers wait impatiently for their dinners. The meat seller and his apprentice busy themselves cutting up meat, slicing up onions, stoking the fire, sharpening one long sharp knife against another, the metallic sound reverberating into the night.

I am at a loss exactly what I am thinking. But I go on thinking nonetheless.

There is a rattling sound beside me. It has been there all these while. But I am only just allowing it to penetrate my mind. I peer into the darkness to

149

determine its source. I see it now. Someone is busy banging repeatedly, and on the same spot on a disused, uprooted metallic signboard advertising a contraceptive. Gentle bangs that grate on the nerves. I think, Doesn't he get tired banging with both hands, stooping the way he is? Perhaps he is doing exactly what I am doing, passing the time, waiting for the ferry. But he won't be boarding the ferry when it does arrive, that I am sure. I ignore the madman and his vocation and occupy myself with more useful things. It is the girl that I think of now; I don't think of her as a prostitute.

I also think of my wife.

There are commotions all around me. I start violently. The ferry has arrived, I notice. Passengers on it are bailing out of the terminal, rushing to the waiting buses and taxis in the motor park, anxious to be taken to their final destinations. The motor park is suddenly alive. Car and motorcycle engines start up, coughing, spurting, belching poison. Nighttime hawkers, with candle lights expertly propped inside transparent containers in the middle of their trays call attention to their wares in drowsy, sleepy voices. Dust rises to the air, fills it. I smell the clay in it, the fine grit finds its way to my mouth, I spit them out. It is a futile task. The night is suddenly illuminated with tens of headlamps. Dust particles dance before me. Cats and dogs cower, dodge under immobile vehicles; prostitutes and their clients back the lights, continue their negotiation in subdued voices. Passengers, laden with loads shield their faces as they hurry to board the ferry. No one is sure how many more trips it will make before cutting off its engines. Already, it is past nine O'clock.

I look around for the girl, hoping not to see her. I think, She may be washing up. By daytime, she sells oranges. She has a makeshift stall: one wooden table and a low chair. She wears a loose blouse with an open neck. If she bends forward to hand you an orange, you can see her breasts. They are a young girl's breasts, full and fair, robust; the nipples thick as the head of the small finger. She is not more than seventeen. The fool that I am: the first day she handed me an orange, I ended up buying over a dozen. Then she came to me in the night where I dozed in an uneasy sleep. I wanted to send her away. I had not gone with a prostitute before. How would I explain it to my wife if she were to find out? But how could I send her away? Those black nipples! Those vacant eyes!

The cars on the queue come alive. Engines purr and rev. The line begins to move slowly. I engage gears, shift to one, then two. How many metres can I travel before they halt our movement and announce that the ferry is full? I hold my breath. Then hold my brakes. The line comes to a halt. The ferry is full. I have moved less than fifty meters. I am dreading spending the night here again. I don't want anything to do with that girl anymore.

Last time, against my will, she led me to the beach. "The space in the car is too small for lovemaking," she said. I will not shame my wife for the third time. I must board the ferry tonight!

I have been visiting this little boarder town across the sea since two weeks back. Since, I became a salesman. Across the sea is part of my territory. Competition for the product I sell is less stiff here. Competitors don't like to come here because of the fear of spending the night across the sea, away from their families, huddled up in the front seat of their vehicles, being battered by the fierce cold all through the night, being harassed by prostitutes with their smelly armpits and vaginas made dry and acrid by over-washing with alum. Not that the girl's armpits smell. And she is young, her vagina is always wet. I don't mind crossing the sea. I sell over three hundred percent of my weekly target here. I sell at a price higher than the company price; the company doesn't know. I make some nice profit; money that my wife can do with. Not to talk of the extra goodies I cart home: oranges, coconuts, paw-paw. Fruits are cheaper across the sea. My clients across the sea are happy that I can come over and service them. I cut off a lot of hassles for them. They are happy paying the extra price I put on my product. I have sworn them to secrecy.

"Make me an omelette and Nescafe," I say to the tea seller. "Make the Nescafe hot."

I hug myself closer. It is colder now that everywhere is quiet. The ferry has departed. The buses and taxis have cut their engines and lights out. Everywhere is uncannily dark. I sip my Nescafe slowly, letting it burn my mouth, enjoying the warmth it fills my inside with. Out in the distance, the lights of the town across the sea are hazy, surrounded by mists, lonely. People are talking in quiet tones around me. The roast meat shop I left behind is getting ready to shut for the night. I can see the apprentice taking things inside. The sea is as black as soot.

It is past eleven O'clock. The ferry had made two trips since. Yet I am unlucky. I am at the lip of the terminal. Should the ferry make another trip, mine will be the first vehicle to board. But it will not. "Until tomorrow," the officials had said when I cried out, "Can't it take just one more car? My Sedan will fit into one tiny space." But nobody was listening to me.

I think, Perhaps she will not be coming tonight. She favoured me with a generous view of her breasts this afternoon when I went past her stall, engaging myself in aimless stroll. Perhaps she has left town and that was her farewell gift. Or has she suddenly taken ill? I cannot let myself think that. If she were ill... My heart races, even as I will it not to. I am confused. Only if she will come and let me know that she is not ill. Then she can go away. Truly, I don't want anything with her anymore. I am happily married. Flattening my backrest, I prepare for sleep. I wind up my passenger side window after winding up mine. I curl into a sleeping position. I close my eyes, my mind far away, trying to focus on my wife, trying to think of nice things about her but failing miserably, my thoughts always returning to the girl. I am mad with myself. "I don't want to set eyes on that girl anymore," I cry. "She is only a kid; a kid for heaven's sake." I bang my dashboard with clenched fists. Blood pumps in my head. My mouth goes dry. Shame for what I have been doing to that teenage girl kills me. She is less than half my age!

I jerk violently up as two soft raps sound on my car window. I peer into the darkness. Her teeth flashes. I am relieved that she is not ill after all. Now, she can go. I can sleep easy. Two more raps in quick succession and I wound down my glass, prepared to tell her off.

"The cold," she says. She is hugging herself. "It's too much."

That is the time I should have told her, "Go home. Go home to your mama." But I say nothing. I smell the cheap perfume she is wearing. She has never worn perfume before. Her hair is freshly made. I smell the cheap relaxer.

"Can I come in?" she says.

I do not answer, but she is already on her way, on her way to the passenger's door. Might as well spend some little time chatting with her, I think. The night is still young. I open the passenger's door. She steps in, smiles at me.

"Do you like my hair?" she says.

She seeks my right hand, finds it, places it on her hair. I feel the wetness, of oil.

"I made it for you. That's why I am late."

I am shaking. I clutch the handbrake to steady myself.

"Hope you don't mind that I am late?" she says.

She draws closer to me.

"It is just too cold outside," she says. "Hold me. Make the cold go away. Your body is so warm."

She snuggles against my chest; her right hand finds its way into my shirt. She rubs the hair on my chest, squeezes my nipples.

"Hug me tight," she begs. "You have not said anything about my hair. Don't you like it?"

I sigh.

"Let's chat," I manage and say.

"What is there to chat about?" she says. "There is enough time to chat, after. Hug me please."

"The hair," I say. "Did you really make the hair for me?"

"It is nice?"

Thoughts of my wife on the other side of the sea suddenly fill my mind. I picture my dinner, keeping warm above the stove, waiting for me. I picture my wife, anxious, going to the door to check at every approaching footstep, thinking it is me; clutching the rosary, saying one 'Hail Mary' after another for my safety; for my safe return.

"Yes, it is nice," I say.

"You are not angry that I am late?" she says.

"No," I say. "Now that I know why you are late, I don't mind."

153

I remember Syl and other stories

mr. apia akpaka

The night preceding the day I was to begin Primary One at Isu Community School will forever remain fresh in my mind. Me, who normally fell asleep as soon as my back hit the bed. But did I sleep that night? No! The reason for my insomnia was the school headmaster, Mr. Apia Akpaka.

Children hated Mr. Apia Akpaka. Even those who had not yet begun school were conditioned to hate him by those who had. A huge man, he had a clean-shaven head, and a somewhat protruding upper front tooth. It was rumoured that since he was born no smile had graced his leathery, lizard-like face - not even by mistake, the rumour mongers claimed, though they could lay no claim to being Mr. Apia Akpaka's relatives, or knowing when he was born.

All my life, the number of times I had set eyes on this phenomenal Mr. Apia Akpaka could be ticked off on the fingers of one hand. The truth was that like other kids, it was not part of my ambition to behold his hawk-like eyes, which were generally agreed to have the power to make your legs rubbery and weak, like a cripple's; and make your throat run dry, like the back of a bamboo stick in harmattan.* An uncountable number of schoolchildren swore they had, at one time or another, felt light-headed and faint simply by looking into those hawk-like eyes! 'Never look into Apia Akpaka's eyes' was therefore a cardinal instruction: that is, if you wanted to survive at Isu Community School.

Out in the village square, a voice would suddenly ring out, "Everybody look, Apia Akpaka is coming! Run, run for your dear lives!" And like magic, the village square would empty, with kids screaming their heads off as they fled. Such was the terror that Mr. Apia Akpaka evoked!

---

* A North-east trade wind: dry and windy.

Who wouldn't scamper on account of Mr. Apia Akpaka? The story went that on his daily strolls round the village, he cradled his custom-made cowhide whip, the *koboko*, under his starched shirt, ready to slip it out with the speed of greased lightning and teach any mischievous pupil a hard lesson.

If your parents gave you an assignment — say, for example, "Uchechukwu, make sure you wash your clothes and have your bath, and don't forget to fetch water from the stream for cooking dinner" - you were most likely to obey. If you didn't, the chances were that, on your parents' invitation, Mr. Apia Akpaka would come calling that evening with his *koboko*. And your buttocks would catch fire!

It was rumoured that on his parent's instruction, Mr. Apia Akpaka had thrashed a disobedient boy from Umugbor, the next village, until the boy passed out, and was only resuscitated by the ingenuity of the village *dibia*,[*] Mazi Ekwueme. Every child that attended Isu Community School swore by his forefathers that he knew this unfortunate boy. But to the present time, none has pointed out that unfortunate boy. But of course, no one needed to point out anybody to confirm that Mr. Apia Akpaka could commit murder in broad daylight. You only had to see him walk - the ground shook with his every step.

So, now you will understand why sleep vamoosed from my eyes that night. I was going to meet the Devil himself! And if I made the stupid mistake of telling my Ma that, "Look, mama, I don't want to go to school," that would be double trouble, for there was no surer way of inviting Mr. Apia Akpaka to your home than to refuse to go to school. So, like a hungry fledgling, I trembled on my bamboo bed.

**   **

The sleep that had fled was only just returning when I heard our stubborn cocks crowing, *kokrorokooo, kokrorokooo,* and the next thing I heard was my Ma opening my room door and shouting, "Wake up, wake up my son! Today is here at last, the day for you to begin school. I know you will make your poor mother proud." Happily, she began to hum a church song. I swallowed hard and began to pray. I didn't even know what prayer I was saying. But one thing I knew was that I wished Mr. Apia Akpaka would just die! Yes, fall down and die, just like that. That was what befitted a wicked man like him.

---

[*] 'Native doctor' or 'medicine man'.

156

I was luckier than most of my mates starting school with me: my Pa had a Raleigh bicycle, the same age as me. He bought it as a special gift for himself the same day I was born. He told me he had to congratulate himself, even if nobody would congratulate him. The reason for congratulating himself, my Pa told me, was that at last he had a male child after six previous attempts had yielded nothing but *ordinary* girls.

"My son," he always said whenever he was in a happy mood, "I had to make sure my two legs were firmly placed on the wall, and then, I dug really, really deep."

My Pa never got beyond the point of the story where he dug really, really deep because my Ma would suddenly come flying from the kitchen, yelling, "Stop polluting that child's mind with your rubbish and nonsense story, you rotten old man." My Pa would laugh and laugh and laugh until tears ran from his eyes. I always found myself smiling, though whether at my Pa's story or at my Ma's anger, I could never tell. I never understood what Pa meant by digging really deep, or why Ma waited until this part of the story before yelling at him.

**   **

Anyway, back to my story. Thanks to my Pa and his Raleigh, I was the first pupil to get to school. Getting to school early meant that I had saved myself six hot cuts of Mr. Apia Akpaka's *koboko*, a sure thing for latecomers. And they were always so many. I imagined the scene as told over a million times by those who had experienced it:

"Now, steady boy…"

"P-pplease s-sir…"

"I said steady…"

"I beg you sir…with my father's name…"

"I don't care about your father, or your grandfather…"

"Forgive me, sir…"

Thuwaai! Thuwaaaai! Thuwaaaaaai!

"Ah, my buttocks have caught fire, sir!"

"Don't worry! The next stroke will quench the fire!"

Thuwaai! Thuwaaaai! Thuwaaaaaai!

It was rumoured that Mr. Apia Akpaka had developed thick biceps by his daily thrashing duties. My eyes strayed to these biceps as soon as Pa and I stepped into his office. My God, the things were bulging, almost bursting through his starched, short-sleeved shirt. I shivered in my khaki shorts, making doubly sure to avoid his eyes lest my legs became rubbery and weak, like a cripple's, or my throat ran dry, like the back of a bamboo stick in *harmattan.*

On seeing us, Mr. Apia Akpaka, like a bullet, shot out of his cane chair, crying, "Come in, come in, Mr. Okeke, come right in, oh dear me, oh dear me." It was a booming voice. Friendly? It couldn't be! And then he continued talking, telling us, "Sit down, sit down, and make yourselves comfortable, there is a chair over there, boy..."

And I froze!

What had I done wrong? I hadn't even moved a muscle since entering his office. *God save me!* He continued addressing me saying,

"Boy, boy, drag that chair over here for your Da..."

And I was all action. In a jiffy, the chair was where his stubby finger pointed.

"Ah, a strong boy you have, Mr. Okeke," he continued, "fine boy too," and my Pa went and told him that, "Ahhh yes, a fine boy, I agree, but he is very stubborn, all my rubber ropes for tying my rice bags have disappeared one after the other, used to make catapults that never succeed in killing any bird."

And Mr. Apia Akpaka's face clouded suddenly, and he cocked his head to one side. Instinctively, I began a fervent prayer as my eyes spied his *koboko,* majestically resting on one end of his long table as he allowed his hawk-like eyes to bore deep holes through me. He wanted me to look him in the eyes so that I would feel light-headed, and collapse. But, thank God I knew all about his tricks: *Shaaame, Mr. Apia Akpaka! Shaaame!*

"Boy, are you stubborn?" he asked at length, and went on without waiting for an answer, "I hope not. What is your name, my boy?"

"Nwa..." my Pa tried to answer for me, seeing how pale my face had become, and probably remorseful for telling on me.

But Mr. Apia Akpaka would have nothing of the sort, crying, "No, no, let him answer, he is old enough to impregnate a woman, how old is he?"

Thinking that this question was meant for him, Pa's mouth opened again to answer, but Mr. Apia Akpaka closed it for him by booming, "No, Mr. Okeke, you mustn't speak for the lad, he is nearly a man, in the olden days, he would already be eligible for two wives, tell me your name and how old are you, my boy?"

Like the Devil he was, it was just his nature to ask two questions at the same time, I thought. I struggled to make my tongue work, as well as make up my mind, which of the two questions to answer first; my name or my age.

Mr. Apia Akpaka and my Pa stared at me, waiting patiently as my tongue, like a rebel soldier, continued to disobey my simple commands.

"The intransigent attachment!" I cursed. "Why show your true nature at this critical time?"

In my confusion, my eyes narrowed into slits. My green and white checked shirt stuck to my back, and my armpits itched like crazy, as if I had doused them with generous amount of the itchy Devil beans. Who was I to itch them, with Mr. Apia Akpaka gawking at me? And, oh God, I had locked eyes with him by mistake! Already, my legs were turning to rubber, and I was beginning to feel light-headed and faint.

Common sense bade me to sprint out of the office, away from this devilish Mr. Apia Akpaka and home to the comfort of my dear mother's bosom. She would understand, I was sure, for not every mother sanctioned Mr. Apia Akpaka's horrible ways. Just as Mr. Apia Akpaka's face contorted dangerously and I was about to bolt away, my tongue worked, and I croaked, "I am just after seven years..."

Mr. Apia Akpaka roared with laughter- ho, ho, ho, ho! shaking the foundations of his office. I heard the school bell tingle from its nail. My Pa laughed too. I knew he was proud of me. After his roaring laughter had subsided a little, Mr. Apia Akpaka clasped me tenderly on my shoulder, crying, "No, no, my boy, you are not just *after* seven years, you are just *over* seven years, say it."

And as clearly as I could, I said, "it".

"No, no, no," he cried further, "I mean you are just 'over', not 'after' seven years - say it."

I understood and said, "you are just 'over', not 'after' seven years".

Squinting his eyes, he scrutinized me carefully before saying:"Well, well, that's a good lad, and what is your name, boy?"

"My name is Nwanna Okeke," I replied.

"You are your father's son," he said, bursting into another round of ho, ho, ho, ho. At last, he said, "Well, well, and clever too." Then he rubbed my head tenderly with huge, sweaty palms.

I couldn't believe it! To be complimented by the legendary Mr. Apia Akpaka, so much so as to have him rub me tenderly on the head? My friends wouldn't believe it. They would say I made it all up. Who has ever heard of Mr. Apia Akpaka, with his leathery, lizard-like face laughing? And his face was not leathery, I thought. At least not the face I was looking at now. If anything, it was fleshy and robust. And friendly too! Suddenly, my legs were no longer melting under me, I noticed, and my light-headedness miraculously disappeared into thin air.

Mr. Apia Akpaka's friendly, booming voice brought me back from my reverie. "Now, now, now," he said, suddenly drawing himself to his full six feet and instantly meaning business, "we had better register you now, Master Nwanna Okeke."

He dragged out a big book I later learned was called a 'Register' out of a table drawer. He asked every question under the sun and my Pa and I answered as best as we could. Where we had no inkling to the answers like, "What year were you born, Mr. Okeke?" And, "What year was your wife, Mrs. Okeke born?" And, "What foods are your family allergic to?" Mr. Apia Akpaka simply provided the answers himself.

At last, he closed his big book, and a large smile beamed across his face. It was a remarkable smile, breaking open like the sun after a bout of heavy downpour.

My heart warmed. I was no longer afraid of Mr. Apia Akpaka. As my Pa and I stepped out of his office, I kept thinking: all those stories about Mr. Apia Akpaka... all those rumours...all those yarns...

"Well, well, well," I said aloud, "devil take all gossips and slanderers!"

Something told me I would enjoy learning at Isu Community School.

my friends come and go

The huge whispering pine trees in my village square stand tall and empty - all six of them. I think they were purposely planted like that: in a circle. As gentle breeze caress their scaly branches, they whisper merrily, dropping dead leaves, sharp as needles. The ground around them is thick with fallen leaves, black and warm from rotting.

Hopefully, I examine the topmost branches, praying to see soft, slight movements, of my friends, the weaverbirds. I see nothing. I don't mind too much. It will not be long before they start arriving.

I have always loved weaverbirds. My first memory of childhood is of sitting on the wet ground, cross-legged and gazing into these magnificent pine trees, wide-eyed, absorbed and thrilled as I watched them carry on their daily activities; thousands of them shrieking endlessly as they played, fought, mated.

I watch them begin the intricate process of building their nests. I am amazed as they round it off, three, four or six days later; how soon depends on whether palm and coconut fronds, their most important building materials, are available or not. When they aren't (this is after they have stripped the nearby palm and coconut trees of all elements of fronds, leaving them naked), the birds fly as far away as possible in search of them. They then ferry long, thin, green strands, expertly sliced with black, strong, pointed beaks, sharp as razor back to the pine trees. I feel sorry for the nearby naked palm and coconut trees. It is the worst part of the year for them, when my friends, the weaverbirds come.

But I will rather the nearby trees remained naked all year long than not see my weaverbirds. It is breathtaking watching them manoeuvre their beaks and claws; their heads and wings; their bellies and tails as they passed the thin strand of fronds this way, bringing them out that way in the delicate, but intuitive process of weaving their homes.

I have since identified the beautiful, red and black coloured birds, which shrieked loudest as the males; and the dull, light yellow ones, which allowed themselves to be climbed on, with semblance of irritation on their demeanours as the females.

There is nothing I enjoy more than watching the weavers shriek, especially in the afternoons when the sun is blazing in the cloudless sky, fit to roast. Then they leave their pine trees and hide under the dense leaves of the mango, pear and malaria trees found everywhere in my village. Their shrieks, rising and fallen in crescendo as they strive to outshine each other leave me feeling drowsy. And suddenly, the birds are quiet, as if commanded. And the entire surrounding acquires a disturbing sereneness, as if a ghost had just strode past.

When they resume, they do so with renewed vigour. Finally tired of vibrating air through their lungs, they fly to the nearby palm trees to feed on the red, shining palm nuts. Or, to the farmlands nearby where they will wreck havoc on the maize plants, bent double with ripe cobs.

Always, I tail them to the maize farms. Or, find a spot a little distance from the palm trees. There, I stand. It is un-quantifiable pleasure, watching them undertake the difficult task of peeling off the covers of the maize cobs with their beaks and claws, their red eyes alert, roving, darting this way and that. They know that the farm owners are only a shriek away. Finally, the maize cobs are peeled, exposing white or yellow seeds, or a combination of both. Hungrily, they feed to their satisfaction.

Whether they are tearing away at maize cobs or plainly feasting on red, ripe palm fruits, the weavers are a beauty to behold. Especially so when they rush to the water hole, a short distance from their pines to water themselves, flapping their wings merrily in the stagnant, sometimes green, sometimes brown water.

As they hop out, wet, to stand in the sun to dry and preen themselves, they open their throats and sing the sweetest songs ever (songs of love, I suppose) to each other.

I close my eyes, lost in eternal bliss, never missing a note.

I will pray that they never stopped killing me. But I know it is only for a couple of minutes before their leader gave the signal. And then they will rise to the air. This time, back to the whispering pines. Or, to the undercover of the mango and orange trees where they will sing and sing and sing their heavenly symphony never seeming to end.

It is the younger birds, the ones whose glossy wings reflect and shimmer against the morning sun that do the most singing. They must secure their mates before the season is over. The older birds, already coupled didn't sing much. Instead, much attention is given to nest weaving. Couples build the nest, in readiness for their eggs. Eggs arrive before the heavy rains come, in July.

Weavers lay about three or four eggs. After the eggs are laid, the females spend more time in the nest, only going to the maize farm or palm trees once or twice a day. In a matter of a week and a few days, the eggs hatch into young weavers, naked and blind to the world.

I have seen the birds after they hatch. Not by climbing the tall pine trees, which are too tall for a boy of eleven, like me. But, when the unfortunate happens, for example, when the wind blows too hard, or when it rains heavily at night and the nests are blown down.

I will wake up the next morning to find several nests lying on the ground, most upside down, soaked. Searching them will reveal eggs, either newly laid, or in advanced stages of incubation, some cracked, some intact. Or young weavers, blind, naked, hairless and helpless, with tummies protruding and legs raised as they struggle on their backs, cycling in the air, beeping wimpy sounds that shred my eleven year old heart. In the absence of their mothers, these fledglings are attacked, killed and hauled underground by battalions of soldier ants.

That is how I came to hate soldier ants so much.

I am powerless against the bigheaded ants. And the elements. I can only pray that the heavy rains stopped. Or, the winds reduced their anger. Or, that when they fell, the fledglings are old enough for me to nurse.

Not minding the lice, which crawl over them in multitudes, I take them home under my shirt, and put them in my cage of coconut bamboo, which my father built for me before they came and took him away in the night and I never saw him again.

My mother helps me make a fire, silently. I warm the young birds by the fire. As they tremble and beg for food with mouths open, I throw particles of bread, or rice or fish; in fact, anything I can lay my hands on, I through into their open, yellow mouths. Sometimes I give them sugar, or pepper. Or even Ovaltine I rummage from castaway tins in the public dustbin. When I am unlucky, these birds die in my care, mostly from diarrhoea.

I am left sad. And heart-broken. Like that time my father went away. He didn't even say goodbye to me. Or, to my mother. Neither did he take his pen and writer's notebook. He just went quietly with the men, and they became one with the black night, the wind howling, the dogs barking.

"The Chief's men," my mother said when I asked her who the men, dressed in black, wearing hoods, were. She said she had been expecting them for a while. No one ever told me what my father did, though I did hear snippets of discussion, adults talking about how terrible the times had become. How one can no longer give a personal opinion of anything anymore; how one can no longer call a spade a spade.

Severally though, I have been lucky enough to adequately care for some of the downed weavers. I return them to their whispering pines after they have grown stronger and can manoeuvre from branch to branch.

I watch them fondly as they make their way to the topmost branches to join their kinfolk. Sometimes, I wonder, *Do these birds I have nursed ever remember me?* But that is the least of my worries. What kills me with apprehension are the killer kites, which first appear as black specks: black stains against the clear white, soothing sky.

They come toward the ends of the rains. Whenever I see them fanning out in the sky, I feel a sudden tightness in my throat and emptiness in my stomach. Whenever these kites show face, two things are bound to happen.

One:

My weaverbirds will no longer sing. If they sing at all, they do so with their hearts in their mouths. You will hear the trembling in their notes. Their songs are no longer melodious, but melancholic, filled with fear, and uncertainties; punctuated with warning signals from one or two who serve as lookouts, risking their lives, exposed at the pinnacle of some tall trees. When they go to the maize farms and palm trees, instead of seating majestically on things, they hang underneath the cobs and bunches, with their wings neatly folded, eating hurriedly; never chatting to each other as they sample opinions about taste and freshness of their meals. The kites, with their telescopic eyes must not sight them.

Two:

Out of nowhere, the kites pounce on the weavers in the whispering trees as they mind their business. And the air will be filled with a mirage of brilliant colours, dirtied here and there with specks of dirty black, several thousand wings scattering in all directions as the weavers run for dear lives. Inside nests, confounded fledglings hold their tongues. Perhaps not the whole story, but even they know something about the enemy kites. The colour of their feathers, for example.

A weaver is pounced upon in flight, at the peak of his life. The kite makes away, to a solitary meal. Or, to feed its offspring, somewhere in the forest, at the top of a silk-cotton tree or a towering mahogany. Or, to just simply maul an innocent weaver for the fun of it, for lack of something better to do; for game.

The kite invasion signifies the end of the migration season. And soon, my friends, the weaverbirds must vacate their temporary home, the whispering pine trees in the centre of my village. They must return to

where they came from (I have often wondered where).
One morning, they begin to disperse. First in small numbers, then in droves. Leaning dejectedly against a small tree, I watch them, several young males and females, not two months old ready to make their first and perhaps most important life trip. Tears well up in my eyes. I don't bother to wipe them. They drop, splashing on my shirt, or making it all the way to the ground, growth of young grasses breaking their fall.

Three or four days later, I am still there to watch the last and youngest birds stretch their wings, and take off. Because they have not made this journey before, I shout as I point out the right directions for them, urging them on, wishing them safe journey.

My mother pleads with me, but I reject food. For days I do nothing but weep. Like that time when men in black khaki uniforms, wearing black hoods came and took my father away in the dead of night, the wind howling, the dogs barking.

I console myself: In only a matter of a year's time, my weavers will be back again, in their annual migration. In time for stripping bare the palm and coconut trees, which would have grown new fronds.

Patiently, I begin to wait. As I continue to hope and pray. I believed my mother when she said, "You Pa, he may surprise us one day and come back home."

The End.